THINKING OUT LOUD

S.A. SARKY

Copyright © 2023. All rights reserved.

With the exception of non-commercial uses permitted by copyright law, no part of this work may be reproduced, distributed or transmitted in any form or by any means, including photocopying, recording or other electronic or mechanical methods, without prior written permission of the author.

This is a work of fiction. Any references to historical events, real people, real companies or real places are used fictitiously. Names and characters are products of the author's imagination and any resemblance to actual persons, living or dead, is entirely coincidental.

ISBN: 9798869957085

For G.

The most honest human I have ever known.

For Stanislow.

I love you for your savage honesty.
 Never stop thinking out loud.

For my daughter, Ava.

I miss you.
Like an unlit candle misses its flame.

It's discouraging to think how many people are shocked by honesty and so few by deceit.

Noël Coward, *Blithe Spirit.*

ONE

The Event

Someone might have known how it happened. Someone might have known why it happened. But without knowing who that someone was, rumours caught fire and spread like an unstoppable, raging pandemic.

Routinely cautious scientists speculated blindly. For once, they couldn't help themselves.

Religions had it figured out, of course. Each one had their own, peculiar version of divine intervention. To them, it was obvious. It was god's punishment. Or blessing, depending on the outcome.

No end of knotted, improbable theories were concocted in bars and pubs, drowned in expensive beer, cheap wine and millions of angry inner voices.

Telepathy on a global scale.

An entire species.

Homo Sapiens, spontaneously, instantaneously, at the same, precise moment in time, unable to keep their thoughts inside their heads. Everyone able to hear what someone else was thinking, as if they were saying it out loud.

The latest trending conspiracy theory put it down to AI, the way it had accelerated our experiments in neurotechnology to the point where we'd cracked the code of human brain waves. With the right equipment, it was now possible to spy on someone's innermost thoughts. Our emotions, our intentions… the way we made decisions… there were algorithms that could work it all out and translate it into words.

They weren't making it up, either.

"Google it," was usually how supporters of the theory would wrap up their argument, sitting back smugly, as if the phrase meant "read it and weep, bitch". But they always seemed to deliver that dénouement before answering the question of how the tech had somehow been unleashed on all of us, all at once.

The fact of the matter was… no one had a fucking Scooby.

After the initial shock, the public outcries, the personal fallouts and the PTSD, the brains of the outfit went to work desperately digging… clawing for the cause, so some kind of remedy could be found. Anything to stop the maddening, psychotic voices.

Drugs.

Trials.

Fails.

Nothing.

Nada.

Not surprising really. Trying to figure it out when all you can hear is the wild, intrusive thoughts of the scientist next to you, probably hampered the process a little.

We only knew its limitations. There seemed to be a physical limit on how far away you had to be from someone else for it to happen. They calculated the radial distance in a silent room to be 3.46 metres. Outside that and your thoughts were safe.

That year, social distancing grew by almost a metre and a half and everyone felt the same thing at the same time: there were nine billion of us and the world just wasn't big enough.

TWO

Panic

The day of The Event.
10:17 am.
Somewhere in Essex.

Jamie jammed his thumbs into the pressure points under his sinuses, resisting the urge to grab the iron bar under his seat and crack it across the pig's face.

'You're really gonna do this? You can see how I'm dressed. Black suit. Black shirt. Black tie. Look at the missus. Where do you think we're going? You're making me even later than I was… he's doing it. I don't fucking believe it. Today, of all days.'

Jamie watched the unflappable, uniformed shoulders shrug before a long arm slowly extended a speeding ticket through the car window.

'There you go, sir. Better to get there in one piece than not at all, isn't it? Don't want any more deaths in the family just yet, do you?'

The copper's voice. Do they teach them all that nasally, condescending monotone at Hendon? Jamie's window was on the way up before the crisp white cuff had retreated fully.

The smirking uniform backed away.

Jamie suppressed a blood-vessel-busting scream, 'Fucking filthy cuuuuuuuuuunt!'

'Let's just go,' said Jamie's girlfriend, Georgie, who'd been staring forward into the hedgerow for twenty minutes, knowing nothing would make a difference.

Jamie slammed on the anchors on the pristine tarmac inside the cemetery, popping its skid mark cherry and sending a piercing screech up the slope towards a modest group of mourners, breaking the stride of the priest giving the eulogy.

A few bowed heads stole a glance over their shoulders. Someone looked up at the sky and shook their head.

'Fuck, fuck, fuck, they're already by the grave. Hurry up, Georgie. And pull that skirt down, I can see the top of your fucking stockings.'

The stony grass made Georgie's heels ping, slip and sink on the way up, forcing Jamie to yank her with him by clumsily grabbing the skin under her arm. Any last hope of a dignified entrance evaporated into the air, alongside Georgie's eye-watering howl.

Jamie gritted his teeth.

'Fucking hell, Georgie. Julie would've heard that,' he seethed, before sending an apologetic smile in Eddie's direction.

Eddie and Julie were one of those couples. Solid as a rock to the untrained eye. But a brittle shell with a soft, pulpy underbelly to those in the know.

Julie was in the box. With only thirty-seven years of breath in her. Taken by a heart attack after a double mastectomy.

Eddie was furious. There'd been only a one percent chance of serious complications, they'd said.

Sounded as close to a sure thing as you could get, right?

So, he'd reassured her.

In his mind, he'd steered her into it.

To be fair, to begin with he was pushing against an open door. It was the first place she went: "Get 'em off. Get 'em both off," she'd said to the doc, straight away. But then the enormity of it sunk in and she got worried.

He thought he was saying the right thing to warm her cold feet. But someone had to be the one percent, didn't they?

So, he felt the guilt… badly. Of course, he did. He should have been around more. He'd just refused to believe there was any real finality to it.

Ninety-nine percent.

For fuck's sake.

If he was a betting man, he'd take those odds all day long.

The priest's voice was soothing to Eddie, even though he wasn't registering a word of it.

But then it stopped.

The funeral director gave an imperceptible nod to his pallbearers and they lowered the coffin into the ground.

Eddie watched the last grain of wood disappear below the lip of the grave, flip-flopping between forcing himself to believe she was in there and fantasising about it being empty… Julie popping up from behind one of the headstones with her phone camera and a sick grin.

It would be the shittiest joke ever, but he'd easily take the pitch black, inappropriateness of the comedy right now, way more than reality.

Eddie looked around to find a few pairs of eyes on him. He knew he had to be the first to grab a handful of dirt and look down into the hole.

It always seemed like such a throwaway gesture when you saw it in films. But now he had to do it for real, starting the filling in, burying her under an impossible weight of earth, his knees almost gave in.

He took a step and felt the first one buckle. So, he steadied himself and locked his joints, swaying forward like Douglas fucking Bader. His legs felt like someone else's.

11:11 am.

Maybe it was the way the wind was blowing. It could have been the fact that the closest person to him was his mother-in-law, Doris, sat right behind, while everyone else stood back respectfully.

They certainly weren't in a silent room. And we know now that the 3.46 metre rule only works reliably under test conditions.

Either way, for whatever reason, it was only Doris, staring into the back of Eddie's head as he gently lobbed the first handful of dirt onto her daughter's body, who heard him thinking out loud.

'Julie. My love light. I love you. I'll always love you. I can't get my head around you not being here. I feel so lost. You've always been there for me. You've been my best friend, my therapist, my nurse, my cook, my precious wife. What am I going to do without you?

'I'm just so glad you never found out about the brass. And the coke binges. All those "golfing" weekends. Even when I forgot my clubs that time. I'd lined up three Latvian teenagers, got a banging deal on a two-nighter. And you came running up the road

after my car, struggling with my bag, sweating like a hippo.

'I thought "she's got to twig now". Shat myself all weekend. Thought I'd be coming home to find all my stuff in the street, burning. I could barely get it up. Actually, that might have been all the gear... But you didn't, thank fuck... Sleep tight baby girl. Always and forever.'

Doris was a pale old bird. But now she was almost transparent. Paralysed, her eyes darted around the graveside at all the sombre faces. They were calm as you like. Why wasn't anyone shouting? Why wasn't anyone doing anything? Why was this wanker still standing? She had no idea how low her jaw had dropped.

As Eddie turned to walk away, it took all her strength to angle her head enough to see his expression. He looked sad. The fucking two-faced cunt.

Then her eldest, Susie, stepped up to the pile of earth and took some. Susie stared straight at her with tears in her eyes, but all Doris could hear, coming from her only surviving child, was sniggering. Like a schoolgirl. Like a bully. Her mouth wasn't moving but it was definitely her laugh. She knew it too well. She wasn't crying, she was laughing. Hysterically.

What the fuck was this horror show she was suddenly in? She felt half her face go weird.

But then other people started to hear it too. Susie's unmistakable laugh. A falsetto machine gun laugh, with a big, honking snort at the end. They'd all shuffled closer, forming the semblance of a queue.

Susie was enjoying herself, delighted by the thought that she was the only one who knew what she was doing. So, she started playing with the laugh, changing it up, trying different types, like an actor finding the one that belongs to their character.

But it wasn't just in her mind anymore, was it?

And neither was the thought that she'd just had… that the privacy of it was so much of a thrill.

By the time half the congregation was within range, she was impersonating Ming the Merciless with a booming *'Muuuuhahahaaaaaaaa!'* as she threw in her handful.

'Fuckin' have that, bitch. You always pissed all over my parades from day one, didn't ya? I know you loved lilies, but I think I'll come back when it's dark

and lay a turd on your grave instead. You might have outshone me, but I fucking outlasted ya. Taddaaa.'

She didn't even notice the gaping mouths around her as she spun around, trying to turn respectfully, but not quite managing the right pace. She was in too much of a hurry to get away, only stopping to give Eddie a brief, "sympathetic" hug. Which he resisted because Susie seemed to be stifling a fit of the giggles.

Eddie didn't have time to deal with it.

Over by the graveside, there were raised voices. One of the lads pushed Jamie so hard, he almost fell in. Georgie was going mental. Eddie stepped between them all.

'What's going on?'

'He just said he wanted to fuck Julie's corpse,' said someone from the back of the crowd.

Jamie started laughing nervously, shaking his head, trying to shrug it off as absurd, 'Did I fuck, Eddie.'

The madness of it wasn't computing inside Eddie's head.

'What the fuck, Jamie? Did you say that?'

Jamie shot straight back, ''Course I fucking didn't.' Then, without moving his lips, *'Well, not out loud. But I thought yeah, I'd do her while she's down there, even without the tits.'*

Eddie erupted. His head drove down onto Jamie's nose, cracking the bone, shattering cartilage and sending a spray of blood across his cheeks.

It was the devil's soundtrack now… real voices and inner voices overlapping… thunderous bellowing, shrieks from every angle, arms thrashing, piling onto and into each other. The desperate priest unwittingly calling for calm before taking one on the temple, dropping spark out, eyes open in the mud.

No one noticed the drool hanging from the limp mouth of the little transparent old lady slumped in the chair by her youngest daughter's grave.

THREE

Epiphany

The day of The Event.
10:34 am.
Somewhere over the Bay of Biscay.

Pat felt another splash of liquid across his cheek and closed his eyes in dismay.

'Jesus Christ, Joan. How many more times? You blathered yourself in the stuff before we took off. I think you're covered.'

Joan reluctantly put the plastic dispenser back in her handbag. Before taking it straight back out and giving herself a final spritz.

'It won't work if you take the Lord's name in vain, Pat. You know that.'

'Holy water, my arse,' Pat spat, before putting down the wet wipe he'd been using to scrape at the coffee stain on his trousers. 'So, OK, I'm game. There's catastrophic engine failure at thirty-five-thousand feet, right? We're hurtling towards the sea at silly miles an hour. What's he gonna do? Wrap you up in magic, so you're the only survivor?'

'Don't be so silly,' Joan said, staring out the window down to the ocean, feeling the vastness of nothing beneath the plane and suppressing the rising fear in her stomach. 'I won't be the only survivor, will I? I put some on you too.'

Pat's eyes rolled. He picked up the wet wipe and started scrubbing again, even more furiously this time.

Joan felt a familiar knot tie itself inside her.

She'd made him angry again.

She'd been making him angry for thirty years.

It wasn't like it was in the books she'd read as a little girl, was it?

And then that perennial thought: Is every couple like this? Was it just her that'd gotten such a bum deal?

She should have kept the bloody holy water for herself.

'Oh, I don't know, Pat. How would I know what he'd do? Anyway, it just… helps me. You can give me that, can't you?'

But Pat had moved on.

The back of his seat kept surprising him with sudden jerks, propelling him forward when he least expected it. Maddening.

He started to wonder how long he'd let it go before he snapped. And decided he'd be justified being on a shorter fuse than usual, seeing as the kid behind was one of the little cunts who'd made him spill his coffee back at the gate.

Gabriel had absolutely no idea about the fumes building up inside Pat's head. He was entirely consumed trying to get Max Thunder to execute a super hammer punch, followed by a power slide and a thunder strike. Why wouldn't he just do it? Jump, Y, forward, forward and Y. Then X and A together. He was doing it right. Why WOULDN'T MAX? He bashed the console hard into his thigh and instantly regretted it.

The stewardess brushed past his arm and filled his nostrils with her scent. It was very different to his mum's sickly perfume. This was exhilarating. He leant into the aisle and craned his neck to watch her walk professionally back to the galley, with all the subtlety of a seven-year-old.

Something confusing stirred in an area around his willy. (It's still a willy when you're seven. It only turns into a cock when your voice breaks.) The feeling was like butterflies tickling his parts from inside. It was new. And he liked it.

But then-

'Excuse me.'

Little Gabby turned to find his entire field of vision filled with leggings.

He slowly raised his eyes up rolls of flab, stuffed into spandex. A cruelly overweight woman was trying to get by.

Terrifying.

He couldn't whip his head back fast enough. But, once she'd crabbed her way past, he couldn't keep it there for long. The urge to watch her wobble to her seat was too overpowering.

'Mum, have you seen how fat that lady is?' Gabriel's face was still pointed in the woman's direction and his volume way too loud for his mother's comfort.

'Shhht, Gabby. We don't use words like fat, remember?' Sarah was well-practiced at using her soothing voice, even when the alarm bells were ringing.

'But she is fat,' said Gabby, his eyebrows scrunched into his eyelids.

'No, she's just got a different body shape to you, that's all. And we don't comment on other people's bodies, do we? That's rude.'

Sarah was pleased with her off-the-shelf response. Thank god she'd read it on someone's blog recently.

She peered through the gap in the headrests to spy on the horizontally challenged lady taking some time to squeeze herself into a standard budget airline seat, next to a couple of twenty-somethings. The girl in the middle smiled extra politely as the woman's folds draped over into her space.

Fuck me. She is a proper lard-arse.

How does someone get that big?

I mean just… would you like another pie? No. The answer is no. I've had three already and I don't need any more, thank you.

How fucking hard can that be?

That poor girl sitting next to her. That'll be a test of her woke level, won't it?

Sarah was sitting between Gabby and his younger brother Cal, after splitting them up to prevent the carnage she could see unfolding as they wrestled and then fought over the armrest.

Rick, their dad, was a dozen rows up after insisting on paying for the extra leg room.

On his own.

A few hours without the pressure of these two.

Bastard.

Next year, she gets the leg room.

Oh, but then he's six foot two, isn't he?

He needs it, she doesn't.

How utterly fucking superbly convenient.

Then she realised she was having a rare moment.

Peace.

No wailing, no tears, no clawing.

There was no point pulling out her phone. That would've been the catalyst for one of them starting up again.

No, she wasn't going to waste it.

She had to tread carefully.

Like a ninja-mum.

A minja.

She made herself giggle with that.

So, she did one of her favourite things: she people watched.

She'd seen a gang of girls get on, some of them still in their hen party outfits. Most of them looked white as sheets. Some of them were minty green. Must have been a helluva week.

God, what she'd do for a little taste of that again.

No responsibilities. What-so-evva.

Apart from getting yourself a bloke and getting yourself home safely afterwards.

It was all she could do sometimes not to pack her shit up and walk out the door. She might as well be a single mum, for all the help she gets from him. Was there a word that was stronger than overwhelming?

She couldn't think of one.

The old man in the seat in front poked his head over the headrest. His face was bright pink and he was shaking. He looked livid. Or was it that shaky head thing you get when you're really old?

'Would you mind asking your son to stop kicking my chair, please?' Pat hadn't intended on adding the please, but the woman's expression made him adapt on the fly. She looked a little broken.

Sarah flipped straight into lioness mode.

'I haven't seen him kick your chair.'

'Well then you must be blind. He's been kicking my chair for the last twenty minutes.'

'Excuse me? I must be blind? Is that what you just said?'

'Look, I just want to NOT have my seat kicked. That's all I'm asking.'

'He's a kid. And he's not kicking it now, are you Gabby?'

Gabby's eyes were back on his game. He shook his head.

'Nope,' said Gabby, without breaking concentration.

Sarah's glare stayed fixed and icy, so Pat retreated.

Fucking hell Rick, thought Sarah. *You should have been here to deal with that.*

Up ahead, she noticed her husband taking something off the stewardess. Was he being a bit too smiley with her?

Rick was loving it. He got to stretch out. Away from the boys for a few hours. And there was a stewardess on board that was proper fit.

He always thought the really good-looking ones got jobs on expensive airlines and eventually got put in first or business. The higher the ticket price, the better looking the crew, right? But this little beauty was on a budget flight and serving him snacks.

Schweet.

And, as if it couldn't get any better, he was relieved to find out he didn't have to sit anywhere near that miserable fucker his kids had been running around at the airport. Just his luck the old man's coffee ended up going everywhere.

They'd announced a delay.

Something to do with, what was it? Additional aircraft preparations?

Whatever that meant.

That's a code though, isn't it?

Why would they tell us the truth? We're just meat on seats, aren't we?

An extra three hours waiting at the gate.

Fucking crap.

What did people expect us to do, with two kids that age and all that pent up energy? They're just children, for fuck's sake. And it had to be the cantankerous old cunt that got it in the end, didn't it?

The stewardess bent down in front of him, trying to dislodge something stuck in a cupboard. He watched her pert backside wiggle as she wrenched whatever it was from side to side, trying to free it. He'd offer to help, but the floor show would be over. So, he sat there letting his cock twitch delightfully. Her arse was just like Julie's, heart-shaped and tight.

Julie.

How tragic was that?

Not much of an innings, was it? Late thirties, something like that. But, if he was being completely honest with himself, it was his Get Out Of Jail Free Card, wasn't it?

It was all easy to begin with. Everything was going so well. He'd learned a lot from his first affair, somehow managing to save his marriage after Sarah found out. This time he'd been a lot more careful. Using a different phone, more obscure apps for texting, not biting off more than he could chew and never cutting it fine. If she found out about this one, it'd be game over. So, this time, he'd made damn sure Sarah didn't have a clue. And neither did Julie's small-time crook of a husband, thank fuck. He'd heard rumours Eddie was a bit of gangster. Someone he shouldn't be messing with. But that was all jumped-up nonsense, wasn't it, surely? This was England, for fuck's sake. And he wasn't living inside a Guy Ritchie film. How bad could he be?

But then came the breast cancer and she'd started getting needy. Talking about leaving Eddie and that. Wanted them to get a place together. What planet was she on? He was a family man. She knew what she was getting into.

Anyway, she's dead now.

One leaky source of stress, plugged.

No more deep, difficult conversations, having to rack his brain to work out what the fuck to say to kick the can down the road again. And he'd managed to get away with it.

Actually, it might even be her funeral today. Shit. Hang on.

Every-man's-uniformed-fantasy was now adjusting her clothes after successfully wrestling the rectangular metal box thing from the wall unit. She pulled on the nylon around her legs and straightened her pencil skirt down and across her hips by smoothing it with both hands. Fucking hell, the things he could do to that.

His internal debate about whether to go to the toilet to relieve himself was eventually decided by the mini brain in his semi-erect penis, which had now gone past the point of no return, "over the event horizon" - as it were - and was fast turning into a full-blown hard on.

Rick stood up with a tactical placement of his hand across his groin, so the woman next to him (and any passenger that happened to be idly looking forwards) didn't twig. He gingerly navigated around the stewardess, angling his arse away so he wouldn't knock her with the now ridiculously obvious bulge in his jeans.

Angie stood up and pointed a well-trained smile in the direction of the middle-aged man dancing around her to get to the toilet, before stopping to take a breath for the first time in the flight.

Service done.

Rubbish done.

Poppy, her crewmate, joined her at the front galley.

'I mean have you ever had to deal with anything like that before?' Poppy whispered out of the side of her mouth.

They were still entertaining themselves with what happened on the approach into Gran Canaria.

'Nope. That was a first,' acknowledged Angie.

They'd been about an hour out when Poppy called her to say there were weird noises coming from the toilet.

Angie had made her way past the queue of people waiting to use it and was about to press her ear against the door when she realised there was no need to.

Coming from inside were the sounds of a wounded animal.

She glanced up at Poppy, just to check she wasn't hearing things. Poppy responded with a shrug of understanding.

Angie rapped on the door.

The noises stopped instantly.

But then a tiny voice, through tears and breathless panting…

'I'm stuck.'

'I'm sorry?' said Angie.

'I'm stuck,' a little louder this time.

'OK. I'm going to open the door, alright?' Angie lifted the lavatory sign and flipped the emergency unlock switch. She glanced at Poppy and nodded towards the passengers standing in the aisle.

Poppy took the hint and started trying to usher everyone up the plane. A few of them stepped back. But the people at the front, who'd been in earshot, weren't going anywhere.

Angie couldn't wait for them to move. The noises had started up again. What the hell had happened for someone to be making sounds like that?

'Please help me.'

She took a deep breath.

And pulled the handle.

Poppy leant back and strained her neck to see around Angie's blazer. The person at the front of the queue almost knocked her over trying to do the same.

The first thing Angie took in were bulging eyeballs on a young man's face. Then the tears streaming down his cherry-red cheeks. Apart from that, it all looked pretty normal for someone sat on a toilet, mid-flow.

But then she scanned downwards and saw that he wasn't sitting normally at all. His bum was lower and his knees were higher than any of those body parts should be.

And his legs.

They were turning blue.

Looking around, she noticed his phone on the floor, recording video.

And the seat was up.

For some reason, he'd decided to sit down on the rim.

'OK, we're going to get you out,' Angie said in her best, reassuring voice, almost following it with "sit tight". 'Give me your arms.'

Like a toddler reaching for his mummy, the lad extended his arms towards Angie. She took them both by the wrists.

She couldn't shift him.

And the harder she pulled, the more pain she seemed to be causing. Poppy got involved and they took an arm each.

No difference.

Angie saw the light on the interphone and picked up. They were starting their descent.

After the co-pilot had come down to see for himself, the consensus was that Angie would stay at the back with the toilet door open, keeping the passenger as calm as possible. They'd get the aircraft on the ground and then call maintenance.

On the approach, Angie grilled the guy about how and why.

Turned out, it was for content.

In his vulnerable, apologetic state, feeling the need to confess and take his mind off what was happening, he let her play back the video on his phone. After a considerable amount of squirming, he'd managed to position himself on the rim to create a vacuum, before hitting the button. Watching the mischievous glint in his eye switch to ice-cold panic as the implosive fury of the flush sucked at his undercarriage, was pretty entertaining to be fair.

Luckily it was a smooth landing.

In the end, it took maintenance dismantling the toilet to get the kid off.

A three-hour delay.

For a hundred and eighty-four people.

For a TikTok.

A call light above row seventeen bonged them back to work. Ah great, the hen party. Looking down the plane, they saw appalled faces across the aisle. Someone gipped.

'Oh god. What is it now?' said Angie.

'It's the shift from hell, isn't it?' Poppy grabbed a roll of clean-up tissue and took off.

11:11 am.

'Let's get that skirt up and pull those knickers to the side. Fuck yeah, I can smell your cunt. I'm putting myself inside you now. Ahhh yeah. Feel that, bitch? You're so fucking wet. You're loving it aren't you? Fucking look at me. Yeah, look at me over your shoulder.'

Rick's thinking was as free and dirty as he could make it, trying to bring himself off quickly in case someone was waiting outside.

The problem was that the person right outside was Angie. And this, all of sudden, was being shouted at volume.

The shock of it threw her completely. As it did the entire front row. Angie was about to bang on the door when she became aware of what else was happening.

The plane had exploded in conversation.

Most of it seemed irritated. A lot of it confused. There was fear, panic, outrage. All at once. Poppy had stopped mopping up the sick on the floor because the instant cacophony was deafening. She was staring back at Angie, looking for guidance while passengers in the seats around her hurled a barrage of vitriol in the direction of the poor girl who'd thrown up.

Little Gabby had resumed a steady, rhythmic kicking of Pat's seat. And now, without opening his mouth, was singing flatly at the top of his voice: *'SUCK MY DICK. SUCK MY DICK. SUCK MY DICK LIKE A LOLLIPOP STICK!'*

His little brother had his hands over his ears, bawling his eyes out, while somehow managing to scream for his mum at the same time. And Pat was fantasising about caving the kids' heads in, now out loud for their mum to hear.

Sarah's primeval, protective parent brain kicked in. She lurched forward, almost involuntarily, grabbed one of the few tufts of hair on Pat's head and yanked it back with all her adrenalin.

'Touch my kids and I'll fucking kill you!' Sarah shrieked, saliva spraying from her mouth as her hand came away, taking a chunk of raw, white roots with it. The bizarre, split-second thought she had about how weak old people's hair was, added another stream feeding the river of noise.

At the front, Angie was trying to make sense of it all. The woman in 1C was desperately pleading with her to do something, but with her mouth shut.

What the actual fuck?

Her first thought was to let the pilots know, even with the sound of Rick coming hard into a tissue on the other side of the toilet door.

Angie composed herself and picked up the interphone.

No answer from the cockpit.

As she stepped closer to the door, she could hear raised voices from inside. This definitely wasn't right. The pilots' usual daytime-DJ-cheery-charm had been replaced with an unbroadcastable urgency.

She tried again. This time they picked up.

'Erm… we've got a bit of situation back here,' she told them.

'Well, we've got a bit of a situation up here as well. Stansted Control isn't responding.'

'Well, that's not entirely accurate,' the co-pilot chimed in. 'There isn't one person talking to us, there seems to be a few.'

'We'll try other flights in the area,' the pilot said, irritated by the interruption. 'We'll see if they're having the same problem. You deal with the passengers.'

Just as Angie was returning the receiver to its cradle, she heard an argument ignite between them, so she brought it back to earwig.

'Brilliant. You're picking this moment to split hairs. They might as well not be responding for all the sense we're getting from them.' Then a just audible, *'Twat.'*

Back in row twelve, Joan was silent. Listening to a church podcast her daughter had downloaded for her, she'd walled herself into her personal Eden, where there was peace, colour and hope. But the wall had been broken by a woman's hand coming over the seat and snatching at her husband's hair.

Joan took out her earbuds.

'Whatever it was you said, Pat, you probably deserved it,' she thought out loud.

Pat was more upset by losing precious hair than the sting of it coming out.

Joan straightened up in her seat, looked past him and around the cabin. There were suddenly voices coming at her from every direction, even though she couldn't see any mouths moving.

The big lady she'd noticed getting on, was now in floods of tears. It looked like the young woman next to her was trying to console her but whatever she was saying seemed to be making it worse. The expressions on the faces of the crew weren't what you'd hope to see as a passenger looking at them for reassurance. Some poor lass had chundered and the rows around her were loudly voicing their disgust… but with their mouths firmly shut. A stewardess was standing in the aisle looking helpless, holding tissue caked in diced carrots and swearing like a soldier but, again, Joan couldn't see her lips parting to speak the words.

So, her brain took a stab at what was happening.

She could hear other people's thoughts, couldn't she?

Was this the magic that Pat had been teasing her about? She pulled out her dispenser and stared at it. Is this what it would have been like for Jesus? Is this how he knew what was in people's hearts? Had she been chosen? Was this her calling, the mysterious voice of compulsion she'd heard the nuns, that used to teach her at the convent school, talk about? What about the second coming… who said it had to be a man? No, that was silly. Don't get ideas of grandeur, Joan. She was most likely just filled with his holy spirit. Either way, there were people who needed her even more than her husband. Pat could fight his own battles.

Joan rose from her seat, dispenser in hand, shifted past her husband and moved gracefully up the aisle, anointing everyone with her water.

Up ahead, Rick tippy-toed from the toilet. The walls had shielded him from the stampede of voices.

The heads of the people in the front row spun around in unison to greet the bemused middle-aged man who looked like butter wouldn't melt in his mouth.

FOUR

Heartache

The day of The Event.
9:54 am.
Addenbrooke's Hospital, Cambridge.

Sagaren Masih was on a break. Getting through a withering spinach and limp cheese torpedo in the hospital café.

In stark contrast to his sandwich, Sag had a delicious face. Chiselled bone under an unblemished coating of skin, like a god had mirror-glazed a chocolate cake. Sharp, clean lines softened by kindness. But, despite his looks and caring temperament, Sag's confidence barrel had always been so empty, it was dry.

When he wasn't scrolling, he wasted time imagining the nurses swooning over him as he proudly strutted the corridors with a consultant's title on his name badge.

Instead, it read: CF Clinical Nurse Specialist.

He was a failure.

Sag loved his job, but he'd come to realise that his parents didn't care how he felt about it. He hadn't got the grades for medical school; it was as simple as that. It didn't seem to matter that he was still devoting his life to helping people. He'd even hoped that getting a posting at a Cambridge University Hospital would carry some weight and fudge the issue enough for them to be proud of him... but nope, it hadn't made the slightest difference. He knew now that, for them, it had always been about the prestige of the position.

With another half hour to kill, Sag inevitably wandered back in time to a previous life.

Dragging his family out of poverty as a textiles entrepreneur, his father had made enough to send him to St. Peter's, a Jesuit-run private school in the foothills of the Himalayas.

His mother? She never said much about it. How much of a say she had in whether he should be sent away as a boarder at the age of six, he never really knew. But he suspected they were both complicit in the plan: for him to become a doctor in the UK. So, St. Peter's must have seemed like the perfect trajectory.

From his childhood home in Chandigarh, it was a relatively quick train to Delhi, then an excruciatingly slow train to his school in the clouds. A two-day, one-way trip. And he hated every fraction of every second because of what was at the end of it.

Knuckles rapped with a ruler for the slightest mistake in a piano lesson. Even with his young, developing logic, the absurdity of punishing someone for not playing well by diminishing their chances of playing well, wasn't lost on him.

Repeatedly shoved into a boxing ring to have the shit beaten out of him, under the pretence of that being the best way to learn how to defend himself.

Returning to his thin wire bed in a crowded dorm, blue and battered by hockey sticks given to kids who didn't have a clue how to use them on the field.

Needless to say, nothing he got "taught" in that endless extracurricular torture, meant he'd be taking on Anthony Joshua, duetting with Alicia Keys or troubling the scouts for the British hockey team any time soon.

He was fourteen when he ran away. Him and another lad he'd managed to tip over the edge to go with him. They'd snuck out before it was light and headed down the mountain. By the end of the afternoon, they'd gotten as far as a gate in the road with some kind of guard post. The guard wasn't stupid. He knew where they'd come from. But it was too late to get them back. So, they were put up in his hut for the night.

The floor space was tiny. Neither of them could stretch out enough to lay flat, so they curled up and eventually exhaustion got the better of them. They both slipped into an uncomfortable sleep, grateful for the shelter, chuffed with their progress and with no idea they'd be marched straight back to school the following day.

Sometime in the night, Sag woke up to a "pooking" sound coming from outside. It was something he'd heard before and he searched his memory to place it. There was a vague recollection there of a family trip into the country… a walk in the forest… the sight of these gentle creatures that his dad told him were Sambar deer. That was it. They made a "pook" sound. Sag relaxed into the idea that there were deer foraging around outside and he drifted off again.

Only to be jolted back into consciousness by frantic scratching on the wood of the door. Sambar deer didn't have claws. What the fuck was this?

He didn't need to rouse his friend. The sound had woken him first because he was propped up against the door. Even in the darkness, Sag could see how wide his friend's unblinking eyes were. His own eyes felt like they were about to pop out of their sockets, as his brain desperately told them to let more light into his retinas, to grab even a fraction more of the moon's reflection coming through the window above.

As the scratching got heavier and more urgent, the boys' breathing got shallower and quicker. Huddling together, Sag could feel that they weren't just shaking, they were convulsing with terror.

The scratching went on. And on. And on. Whatever this animal was, it wasn't giving up.

And then splinters started firing around inside the hut. And then they could see the tiger's paw and the claws that came with it. And Sag was horrified at the size of them.

The first time the tiger's front leg came through the gap, his friend lost his shit and clambered over Sag to get to the back wall. The second time it came through the door, it scraped down the back of Sag's right thigh and across his calf, sending searing, agonising pain from his leg through his entire body so intense that even the skyrocketing adrenalin wasn't enough to keep it at bay. That thing that people talk about when something terrible is happening to you… that thing where time changes and everything switches to slow motion, like seeing the world through the eyes of a fly, Sag now knew this was true. It was impossible to anticipate when the next slash would come, but he managed to flip his body around, so he could kick out when it did. The tiger had already switched tactics though, returning to its incessant scratching, even more violently than before, as if it knew the door wasn't far away from collapsing enough to let it in fully.

The two boys waited to die.

Sag had time to think about what it'd be like, being ripped apart by claws and teeth. Would it be painful all the way through? How long would it take?

At what point would death come in that process? Interesting questions for a fourteen-year-old brain to have to consider.

And then a pop sound. And another. And shouting. And the scratching stopping. And the door flinging open. And Sag squeezing his eyes shut, waiting for the first piercing of his skin. But it not coming. Just the panic in the voice of the guardsman, his radio crackling into the purple night air and the feeling and smell of warm, metallic liquid leaking from Sag's body onto the tiny floor of the hut.

He supposed it took his mother's hysteria (where did all that come from, all of sudden) for his father to finally pull him out of hell and ultimately put him on a plane to England. "Fine," he'd said. "Get yourself into the British system and don't let us down."

He didn't remember much being discussed about the actual attack. It all seemed to be about him running away.

Much later, he discovered that tigers sometimes mimic the sounds of their prey before an ambush.

Sag took a last, reluctant bite of cheese, bread and spinach and winced as he habitually rubbed the raised scar on the back of his leg.

Lilly would be in soon. Which meant that Angie, her mum, would be here too.

Even better, it was the first day of Lilly's annual review, so he'd get to see Angie for longer than usual. Even though she never gave him anything to latch onto, somehow, he didn't feel quite so alone when she was around.

As Sag cleared the crumbs with his napkin and placed the chair neatly back under the table, his kind smile returned, wiping away the twisted expression he didn't even know he'd had on his face, all through his break.

A lady in the queue, clutching the same sandwich, had been watching him and concluded that it must have been truly awful, so she quickly changed hers for a pasty.

Lilly arrived at the clinic on her own. Sag was waiting.

'Hi Lilly, how you doing today?' he asked brightly, professionally compressing his eagerness into cheerfulness. He looked back through the doors over Lilly's shoulder, 'Is your mum parking the car?'

'Hey Sag!' Lilly said buoyantly, matching Sag's bounce with her own. 'Nope, she's not coming 'till later. She's flying at the moment.'

'Oh. Er… OK. Then how did you get here?'

'I got the bus,' replied Lilly, as matter-of-factly as she could. 'I know. She's never missed a check-up, let alone a review. She tried but she couldn't switch her shift this time. I suppose it was going to happen eventually.'

'And you got here all by yourself?' Sag made sure he showed Lilly how impressed he was. 'Well, I suppose you're a young woman now. What are you, sixteen?'

'Saaaag. Stop being silly.'

'You never cease to amaze me, young lady,' said Sag. And, after a brief, disappointed glance back through the clinic door, he led Lilly down the hall.

'I bagsied you the best room in the building,' Sag announced, as Lilly followed him into a room as bare and clinical as every other she'd been in over the years.

Lilly looked around theatrically, 'Wow, I can see that. Thank you soooo much. You really shouldn't have gone to all this trouble.'

'You're very welcome m'lady,' bowed Sag, giving her his best butler impression. 'Wait. You may scoff, but...' he whipped open the hospital blue curtains. 'It's a room with a view.'

Lilly walked to the window and looked out onto the damp, grey car park.

'Well... what can I say? It's stunning,' she smirked.

'Did you bring your PEP mask?' Sag asked, as he began reading down the checklist of everything that needed covering. From her backpack, Lilly had already retrieved the ugly device she used at home to help her clear the mucus from her lungs and was holding it out for Sag, along with a Tupperware box and some paperwork.

Sag looked up.

'Of course, you did,' then, taking each item in turn, 'And your medication. And your food diary. And a consent form. Excellent. Belt and braces. I wouldn't have expected anything less from you. OK. So, as you know, it's going to be a bit of long day. We've got the usual lung function and oxygen sats measurements to take. A chest X-ray, bloods, a bit of physio, a chat about what you've been eating and a bone scan. OK?'

'You forgot the ultrasound,' Lilly prompted as she emptied the rest of her bag neatly onto the side table.

Sag looked at her under his eyebrows.

'And an ultrasound of your abdomen. I was just testing you.'

'Well, I passed then, didn't I?'

'Yes, you passed. You always do. With an A star.'

While the bants had been bounding around, Sag had shrewdly been paying attention to Lilly's appearance. She looked a lot thinner. He needed to check her sugar levels.

'I'm also going to give you this to pee in, OK?'

'Sure,' Lilly said as she took the sample bottle. 'Mum said she'd be here about two o'clock, at the latest.'

'Great. Well, you know the drill. Make yourself comfortable. I'll be back in a bit.'

Sag softly closed the door on his way out.

Lilly was three years old when she caught a cold that wouldn't go away.

Eventually, after a raft of tests, she was diagnosed with Cystic Fibrosis, an inherited condition that, without getting too medical about it, causes a whole heap of shit for a young body to deal with. Aside from the typical lung problems, the list of new, surprise ailments that Lilly had had to deal with over the years had been endless, as one complication led to another problem in yet another organ: bronchiectasis, emphysema, pancreatitis, diabetes, malnutrition, bladder issues, stunted growth.

And the severity of her condition meant that there would, almost certainly, be more to come.

Because her mum's work took her away for days at a time, Lilly had learned how to check her own glucose levels and give herself insulin injections at home. She had to clear her airways regularly, so the build-up of mucus didn't cause any more infections. The frequent check-ups and the constant need to monitor her liver and bones meant that, at the tender age of twelve, she'd spent more time in hospital than most people in their nineties.

This was a life sentence.

And there was no cure.

While all the tests, the prodding and the poking were normal for her, she was all too aware of how other kids had never had anything remotely close to deal with.

She had her moments of raging envy. But somehow, she managed to keep them in check.

Maybe it was because she'd never known anything different, but the inevitable depression that reared its distorted head every now and then, that would have crippled an adult, she'd grown used to taming.

Lilly was a remarkable kid.

Way wiser than her years.

A strong mind and a huge heart, caged in a puny, delicate shell that was impossible to escape.

She was sharp enough to realise that, while her body would never grow like other people's, she could grow up quicker than other kids her age. She could control how her mind developed.

Joining social media groups with other kids living with chronic conditions gave her some support. She realised there were people like her out there, dealing with a whole load of crap, but to look at them you'd never know.

And while she doesn't remember her dad ever being in the picture, her mum had always been there, right next to her. So much so, Lilly recognised, that she'd given up her own life to take care of her.

Lilly resented catching those glimpses of nihilistic panic flash across her mum's face as a new diagnosis came in, almost instantly erased by the face of strength she switched to when she looked at her. Her mum deserved to be happy.

Lilly was forever conscious of the fact that she'd always be the deepest source of anguish, sadness and pain for her mother. Which is what drove her appreciation for the sacrifices she constantly made without hesitation. And Lilly desperately wanted to give back. She'd come to the conclusion that if her mother had another soul in her life, it would give her a chance at a life, beyond Lilly, beyond the reach of this cruel disease that dominated everything.

Especially for when she was gone.

If she could help make that happen, then she'd at least feel a degree of satisfaction that, in some small way, she'd been able to contribute to her mum's happiness, to mitigate the stress she dumped on her every day.

Lilly had watched her mother dip her toe into the dating pool with horrible results. Coming out of each encounter emptier and more exhausted than before. So, her mum had given up. And ploughed every last ounce of effort and energy into Lilly's world.

So, the way Lilly saw it... if dating apps caused more harm than good... she was going to find another way for her mum to meet her soulmate. And being here today was the opportunity she'd been looking forward to.

Something in the way that Sag changed around her mother, gave her a feeling that there was something behind the polish of his bedside manner. And she couldn't think of anyone better to give her mum a chance at peace and stability.

Sag appeared with the gubbins for the cannula.

The timing, Lilly thought.

As he settled onto the stool next to her bed, she hatched her little plan.

'You know, my mum talks about you a lot.'

'I doubt that very much,' Sag mumbled, before remembering who he was talking to and regaining his composure. 'Really?'

'Yeah.'

Lilly waited for Sag to open up the conversation, but he'd been completely broadsided. Whenever a compliment came his way, especially if it might lead to an opportunity for a relationship or a new, exciting connection in his life, Sag became a terrified little boy cowering in a guard hut with a tiger at the door.

'Yes, really,' insisted Lilly. 'She's always talking about how kind you are. She thinks you're really nice.'

'Aww, well that *is* nice,' said Sag. *Nice guys don't get the girls though, do they?* 'Which arm today?'

Lilly extended her left and turned it so Sag could find a vein. This was going to be tougher than she thought.

'Well, it's not just that she talks about you,' Lilly continued. 'I've seen the way she looks at you.'

The needle froze just above Lilly's skin.

'What do you mean?' Sag couldn't look up. He had to keep focused on his job. 'Here it comes, just a little scratch,' and the needle was in. 'How was that?'

'You're the man, Stan,' Lilly said. 'Didn't feel a thing.'

Sag smiled softly, relaxed Lilly's hand and let the red, black blood flow into different coloured test tubes, before taking more time than usual tidying and taping the cannula on Lilly's forearm.

'I mean... I see the way she looks at you,' said Lilly, repeating herself but emphasising every word this time. 'She really likes you.'

'Well, I like your mum too, Lilly. She's lovely.'

Sag was now struggling to maintain a professional distance. Like a lovestruck teenager, he was desperate to get into it, wanted to hang on every word from Lilly's mouth, to get every last detail about the conversations they'd had about him. Instead, what came out was, 'Did you pee?'

Lilly was now very unsure about what she'd just done, what can of worms she may have just opened. Her mum had never spoken about Sag. She'd never seen her give him any of her attention, apart from listening intently when he talked about Lilly's treatment plan or when he was giving her instructions for what to do at home. This hadn't gone the way she'd hoped.

She passed Sag the now heavy sample bottle.

'Thank you. Now, shall we get you up to X-ray?' Sag nodded towards a chair he'd rolled into Lilly's room.

'Ch'yeah,' replied Lilly, so well-practiced at shrugging off bleak thoughts, at least superficially, she even managed to sound enthusiastic. 'Can that thing wheelie?'

'Let's find out, shall we?'

Sag pushed Lilly into the lift, joining a porter in a mask, checking his phone and leaning against the wall next to a patient trolley. From her low vantage point, all Lilly could see of the human causing the bulge in the blanket was a fragile whisp of blue-rinsed hair and a patch of wrinkly skin. They were out for the count.

Lilly looked up at the underside of Sag's chin, 'I can walk, you know.'

'I know. But where's the fun in that?' Sag said. 'We've got wheelies to pull, remember?' He pushed down on the handles, lifted the front of the chair and made a revving sound.

Lilly giggled.

11:11 am.

Behind the mask, the porter started singing. Well, not started singing, as such. It was like he'd begun singing halfway through a line from a song, mid-lyric.

What was even odder, to both Sag and Lilly, was how loud it was. This wasn't a low humming or a barely audible crooning-in-your-head type thing. This was full-blown, belt it out at the top of your lungs, talent show level. Like he was on stage or something. At that volume, you'd expect his mask to be moving around all over his face, but it stayed precisely where it was. No change in facial expression or muscle contractions of any kind.

'How is he doing that?' thought Lilly.

And then, if that wasn't weird enough, the person-shaped mound on the trolley burst into life. From what Lilly could see, there hadn't even been a change in their position, no stirring under the covers whatsoever.

But, coming from the trolley, they heard an old woman's voice, crisp and clear as you like, *'Oh yes, Arthur, I'd love to dance. Well, isn't this just wonderful? You look so handsome in your uniform, my darling. I do love The Andrews Sisters, don't you?'*

Lilly checked Sag's face. And heard him say *'What the actual fuck?'* without opening his mouth.

Sag took a closer look at the patient. Her eyelids were closed. The only movement was coming from the eyeballs darting around underneath her eyelids.

She was dreaming.

The porter paused his song and spoke to the old woman without looking down or acknowledging her little fantasy.

'We'll be there in a minute, Alice,' he said, just as the lift bobbed to a stop and the doors opened.

He then resumed his singing, gathered up the end of the trolley, pulled it out of the lift, spun her to the right and off down the corridor. The motionless patient now coyly feigning protest at an invisible Arthur getting frisky with her.

'This is us too,' said Sag, wheeling Lilly out and turning in the opposite direction. 'How weird was that?'

As they trundled towards Imaging, Sag and Lilly's minds were quiet. They were completely preoccupied with the snippets of monologue they heard every time someone walked past.

Until they arrived at Radiology.

The waiting area was bedlam. A sound clash of confusion and arguments. There was only a handful of people there, but it sounded like Saturday night in casualty.

The staff behind the desk weren't coping well.
At all.
One of them shot daggers at Sag, then at Lilly.

'Oh, fuck off, not now,' is what they both heard, from an otherwise sweet looking nurse. The rudeness of it made Lilly burst with laughter.

'We're not taking any patients at the moment,' the nurse told them. 'Not until we can work out what's going on.'

Sag wasn't going to argue.

'I'm going to take you back to your room, Lilly.'

He spun a one-eighty and took off.

On the way back, Sag tried to take Lilly's mind off it all with a distracting chat about what the rest of her day looked like, engaging her with their typical back and forth about the physio being a sadist and her psychologist being a crate short of a warehouse.

But he needn't have bothered. Lilly had already worked out what was happening.

And she was dead excited by it.

She used their banter as practice, seeing if Sag would notice that she was talking to him without using her voice.

With Lilly looking forward and Sag pushing from behind, neither of them could see each other's faces. So, it took for them to get all the way back to the room before Sag realised that at some points, he hadn't opened his mouth to talk. He'd just thought something and Lilly had responded.

Or had he just imagined that?

This needed to be tested, so he formulated a sentence in his head, *'Mind your legs on the door, Lilly,'* before shifting his body to the side so he could see Lilly's face and watch her response.

Lilly was having the most fun of her entire life.

Knowing exactly what Sag was trying, she looked at him right in the eyes and thought, *'Thanks Sag. But I can push the door open myself.'*

Sag jumped.

Lilly sniggered.

And she flicked her head towards the inside of her room, inviting Sag in.

Maybe Lilly wasn't frightened because she'd been through so many new experiences with her body, that this was just yet another monumental change for her to deal with. For Lilly, with the agonising unpredictability that CF threw at her, left, right and centre… random was regular.

Maybe it was because she was still a child. She wasn't plagued by the cynicism of an adult. Her imagination was still vivid and rich and colourful and important enough in her brain to interpret what we think we learn through experience as impossible, as not just possible… but likely.

Lilly knew what was going on because she allowed herself to follow the logic and go with it.

'Stay here, Lilly. You'll be safe. I need to go find out what's happening.'

Sag was subconsciously pacing the floor.

'This is… this isn't… nah - there has to be a reasonable explanation - this is a hospital for Christ's sake – there must be someone here who can work out what's going on - not sure where to go, though - who do I talk to?'

'Sag… Sag… it's OK,' said Lilly. 'Calm down. Someone might know what's going on, yes. But I'd like it if you stayed with me for the moment.'

Sag stopped. Took a deep breath and slowly perched on the edge of Lilly's bed.

'Thank you,' Lilly's voice was warm and unafraid. 'Sag… think about it. What do you think's happening?'

'What I think's happening can't be happening.'

'Really? Why?'

'Well, because it's impossible. There's got to be a rational explanation.'

'What's impossible?'

Sag sighed and drew in as much air as he could.

'What, you want me to say it?'

'Yeah, say it,' Lilly nodded.

'It's impossible for a human being to hear what someone else is thinking. There's no evidence for it. Telepathy is not a thing. It's a Hollywood idea and… well, it's just nonsense.'

'And yet, here we are,' thought Lilly. And of course, Sag heard it. Just like she'd said it out loud.

Sag rubbed the tops of his eyes and then his temples.

'OK… OK… I'm aware that, right now, I'd look like an idiot if I argued with you. So, alright…' Sag blew gently through pursed lips, grabbing himself inside by the scruff of the neck. 'Let's deal with what we need to deal with right here, right now. Call your mum.'

Lilly's composure instantly fell away. Her stomach dropped into her feet.

'I can't, she's in the air. Oh my god. She's in the air.'

'OK, so we don't know where this is happening. It might just be here in the hospital. Try her anyway.'

Lilly grabbed her phone and tapped her top favourite.

No ringtone.

Three dead beeps and it threw her back to her home screen.

From the other side of the window, they heard the unmistakable sound of a car accident: a whomp, a crunch of metal and the shattering of plastic.

FIVE

Pandemonium

The day of The Event.
Everywhere.

While a nasty brouhaha erupted at a funeral in Essex, heavy turbulence occurred over the northeast Atlantic and crippling confusion spread through a hospital in Cambridgeshire, spare a thought for the rest of the world.

7:11 pm.
Nyŏngbyŏn, North Korea.

Choi Hyun-woo, a senior nuclear physicist, had the misfortune to be in a late meeting with government officials passing down an order for him to speed up production of weapons-grade plutonium in the Experimental Light Water Reactor at the Yongbyon Nuclear Science and Weapons Research Center.

And, at the precise moment of The Event, was unlucky enough to be musing about how ignorant the Supreme Leader must be to think that maintaining consistent reservoir levels to provide enough water to feed the cooling systems, especially after all the flood damage to the pump houses, was as easy as, what, just working a bit harder?

Then finding himself in a faeces-ridden, windowless cell, facing execution by some whimsical method of complete overkill. His wailing thoughts resounding through the jail, along with countless others.

What was it going to be for him? Obliteration by an anti-aircraft gun? Burnt alive until crispy? Blown to pieces by a shell meant for heavy armour and what was left fed to the dogs?

And then, oh fucking son-of-a-bitch.

His entire extended family would follow.

Great.

Just great.

In the end, Hyun-woo's death would be "D": none of the above.

He would exhale for the last time at the grand old age of ninety-two, in the arms of his wife, surrounded by two generations of his children, after witnessing one of the most epic uprisings in history.

With the entire population's instantaneous inability to suppress their true feelings about the regime... the stress from deprivation, the hunger pains, the agony from the "disappearing" of so many loved ones... it all exploded onto the surface in a single, unifying moment. Twenty-five million people involuntarily broadcasted lucid, ferocious hatred for those responsible.

And, with nothing left to lose, exposure overcoming terror, sacrificing thousands along the way to bullets and shells shot by a confused military resisting the change, protecting their divine ruler or afraid for themselves... the overwhelming majority would eventually take control of their future, riding the sonic wave of their deafening, screaming thoughts all the way to the presidential palace.

Nice one.

4:11 pm.
Omsk.

Mila Popov was beaming. After her fairy-tale betrothal and crowning at Svyatoy Tatyani orthodox church, she was standing with her husband-to-be Aleksei Kuznetsov, in front of the registrar at ZAGS for the rospis v zagse, the civil ceremony that would declare their marriage legal and official.

She just needed to get that ring on her finger and everything else would slide into place too. This would be the first day of the rest of her life, with a new life growing inside her.

It was just that 4:11 pm was exactly the wrong time for her mind to wander to the real father of the child she was carrying, the child that Aleksei had naturally assumed was his and that had prompted his joy-filled proposal.

So, what happened next in that ceremony at the registry office?

What punctured the magic of the day, were these words coming from Mila's head, spat loud and crisp from behind her closed mouth: *'Fuck you, Borya.*

Your kid will never know you because this man's going to take care of him.'

And then Aleksei's brow burying itself into the bridge of his nose as his attention darted from Mila to his mother to his friends to the registrar as he said-slash-thought, 'Sorry, what? *Who the fuck is Borya? This isn't my kid?'* then to Mila's wide-eyed witness, *'Did you know about this?'*

And then the piercing voice of Aleksei's mother, 'I FUCKING TOLD YOU SHE WASN'T RIGHT FOR YOU. I KNEW SHE WAS A BITCH-SLUT. I KNEW IT. I FUCKING TOLD YOU.'

The last "fucking told you" reached Aleksei's ears with a slight Doppler effect as his mum flew past, on her way to pull and scratch and gouge and rip at Mila's hair and skin and eyes and dress.

While they wrestled, it was impossible to tell what was being shouted using old fashioned vocal cords and what was being thought out loud. To tell the truth, in amongst the thumping and the slapping and the grunting, it didn't really matter. Many of the guests had been beyond the 3.46 metre threshold to hear what had sparked the reaction in the first place. Then they were too focused on trying to prise the two women apart to comprehend the enormity of what was really happening.

Every ounce of Aleksei's strength left his body, to the point where his legs couldn't hold him. He crumpled to the floor and sat there at a strange angle, propped up on the one elbow he was able to lock, staring through the mist-grey tiles into oblivion, his mind jump-scrolling to those times, almost a year ago, where Mila had explained away her absence with improbable but just plausible excuses. He'd chosen to lower the red flags every time, desperate to believe the woman he'd fallen deeply in love with. And then the news of the baby, making the anxiety of losing her go away, the security it brought him, allowing him to finally surrender to the love he felt for her. The baby… their baby… HIS baby had given him the green light to go all in.

And now this.

'What a monumental fucking idiot I've been,' he thought out loud from the cold, hard floor of the registry office, his confidence in himself, in humanity, in his whole framework of reality, shredded.

And then shredded again.

The fight spilled into the square outside, where a surprised limo driver was smoking a cigarette. He rushed to flick it to the ground, not wanting to look unprofessional, but soon realised this was one indiscretion that was going to go unnoticed.

The scrum ripped a net of balloons, each one printed with Mila's maiden name, so that dozens of white helium-filled teardrops evaporated into the sky. Straggling Popovs popped as they got caught between concrete and a hard place: the bride and the mother-in-law going at it until they fell awkwardly.

As they went down, Mila's hair clip caught the latch of a wicker basket filled with doves and, as they flapped from their cage, a terrified bird got snared in the last recognisable section of what was, this morning, a meticulously styled hairdo.

6:11 am.
South Boston.

Keelan Clark was delighted to have gotten home early from his paint-prepping night shift at the Tesla Service Centre down in Dedham. He'd found Erin, his wife and the mother of his child, right where he thought (and hoped) she'd be, cooking him a steak for his dinner, while she made herself breakfast.

Erin worked days at the Amazon warehouse up in Revere. She'd seen an ad online asking if she was looking to "unbox her AMAZing".

Who wouldn't want to do that?

So far though, in her role as a Delivery Station Warehouse Associate, she wasn't sure if she'd managed to find her amazing, let alone unpack it. But the work was bearable and the perks were decent.

Given Keelan's new job (hopefully his last) and the daily pattern that had been forced on them as a result, dawn was very much their moment. Crossing each other like proverbial ships coming in and out of Boston Harbor, they'd soon made a point of spending undivided time together over the kitchen table, before their son Brandon raised himself from the dead, Keelan collapsed into their still warm bed and Erin headed out on her twenty-minute drive across the water.

Erin and Keelan were a very rare thing indeed. Two people still in love after twenty years of marriage. Sure, the type of love had changed over time. They weren't as bat shit crazy in the bedroom as they used to be, but they'd replaced the greed for each other's bodies with other physical ways of being close. At least one proper cuddle-like-you-mean-it every day and plenty of reassuring touches. They didn't tell each other they still felt deeply for the other person, they didn't have to. It had gone beyond that. They proved it, by always making themselves available. Showing up, as Americans might call it. Being there, you know. Erin and Keelan were best friends and couldn't imagine life apart.

Living in the same house in Southie as three generations of Keelan's family had before, they'd witnessed the gentrification of South Boston with mixed emotions. They missed the earthy, working-class Irish spirit that permeated the streets when they were young. On the other hand, they were now sitting on a gold mine, waiting for the moment when it felt right to sell up and retire somewhere peaceful out in the sticks. They dreamt of that often and were brimming with brightness and hope for their future.

But, before that could happen, they had to help their son make a life for himself.

Brandon had just scraped through high school. He'd turned eighteen two weeks before but hadn't wanted a celebration. Of any kind. What his parents didn't know was the reason why.

Brandon had no one to invite.

And he sure as hell didn't want to get into another pointless conversation with his mum about this friend and that, whose names she seemed to pluck out of thin air as likely candidates for wanting to be in his company.

"Why didn't he just ask them?" she'd always say.

For fuck's sake. Like that would work.

The only thing those exchanges succeeded in doing was to make him feel more alone than ever. The fact that not even his own family knew anything about his life and his struggle with impenetrable isolation, just compounded the anxiety and propelled him into a downward spiral of fear and self-loathing.

Brandon had tried opening up to his dad and his mum on different occasions, but they just couldn't seem to grasp what he was feeling.

His dad reminded him of everything he'd been handed on a plate, that he just needed to stop overthinking things, man up and get on with it.

And his mother, well, she'd glazed over and fused out pretty quickly, before asking if he wanted something nice to eat to cheer him up.

Both times he'd come out of it feeling worse. So, there was no point in trying it again.

To say there was friction between Brandon and his father would be putting it mildly.

Keelan couldn't wrap his head around why his son was so bone idle, as he saw it. The gap between their generations felt like a canyon, compared to the one between him and his father, and even his grandfather. What had happened to kids these days? They were like fucking aliens. Keelan had almost lost the will to start yet another father-to-son diatribe about him needing to be more decisive about what he wanted to do with his life: "Just pick something you're vaguely good at and aim for it. What's so hard about that?"

But then, Brandon would come back with a "What, like you?" response, slagging off his dad's blue-collar job and telling him he'd never done anything special or different with his life, so who the fuck was he to be lecturing him?

And that would really set Keelan off.

He'd always put food on the table. He'd put him through high school. He'd bought him his first car. He'd saved up a college fund for him. "That's what that stupid fucking blue-collar job has done, you ungrateful little brat. Pick a fucking subject and get your ass to college. Or get a job. 'Coz you ain't gonna laze around here 'til you're thirty, that's for sure."

They'd squared off against each other more than once. And Erin was always terrified that the chest puffing would escalate to something that neither of them could take back.

She'd always jump in at the point when Brandon resorted to having a pop about his dad's height, blaming his genes for being short and weedy. His lot giving him no chance of ever joining the jocks and getting the girls.

She understood that this was more than a sore point for Keelan, that he'd wrestled with it for most of his life, which was why she knew that was the time to intervene.

But, while Erin's soothing tones nipped Keelan's temper in the bud, all they ever did to Brandon was make his cheeks flush with the prospect of tears and send him running to the sanctuary of his room.

Erin told herself over and over that her son, right now, was just a bit of lost soul. And that wouldn't last forever. He was a teenager; his hormones were all over the place. He'd start kicking eventually. He'd find a direction. It would all work out in the end.

And so, they were gob smacked to see Brandon, not just appear at the table at that time of the morning but take his seat wide awake and full of energy. At least in the direction of his phone. They stared at each other and shrugged.

With Brandon's thumbs bionically working the screen, Keelan fell into default mode.

'How many times, Brandon. No phones at the t-' before catching Erin giving him the "don't start" look as she brought their food.

'D'you want some breakfast, Brandon?' Erin asked. 'I've made extra.'

'Nah,' said Brandon without looking up, before realising he needed to add another word. 'Thanks.'

It was then that their atomic clocks turned to 6:11.

As Keelan was about to put the first piece of steak in his mouth and Erin was taking a moment to enjoy the simple pleasure of having both the men in her life around the same table at the same time… *'Today's the day,'* came out loud and clear from Brandon's brain, as he texted his group chat.

'Today's the day for what, baby?' said Erin, cutting a corner off her avocado toast. The bloody thing wasn't soft. How come it was only the avocados that she bought that were either too hard or grey and past it?

'What?' said Brandon.

'What's happening today?'

'Nothing.'

'Oh, it's just that you said-'

'I'm texting, mum. It's private.'

'Oh. OK.'

Erin assumed it had been spoken and Brandon was so buried in his chat and jacked about the day that lay ahead, that it didn't register with him that his mum could never have seen his messages from where she was sitting across the table.

His thumbs continued to quickstep across the bottom of his phone, as his thoughts echoed what he was typing.

'Didn't have enough for AR-15s. Got a Bushmaster M4 Patrolman and an American Tactical GSG-1622 Carbine in my car. Got a dash cam in there. Gonna live stream my bodycam on Rollo. Don't miss it.'

Someone he'd not seen before on the thread chimed in and their message came out of Brandon's head as he read it, *'What you gonna do, shoot up a school or something?'*

Brandon shot back a reply, *'Don't be stupid. You'll see.'* But then he couldn't help rising to it, *'Shooting up a school is fucking lame bruh. Been done a million times. Nothing special now. Watch on Rollo. I'm going for school buses. Take the driver out and get on. They can't run anywhere. Fish in a barrel. Back in my car. On to the next. Take the po-po a while to catch me if I'm on the move. Reckon I can do five, maybe six buses. Going for the record. Going bus-hunting bruh.'*

Keelan was like concrete. The only thing he moved were his eyeballs in Erin's direction. She was already trembling in disbelief. The fork dropped from her fingers and fell perfectly upright in the avocado. She couldn't do that again if she tried.

'Stay there,' Keelan mouthed the words silently to his wife, but they came out anyway.

Brandon was still too involved in his screen to notice his dad slipping away from the table.

Erin's mind was numb as she watched her husband disappear through the door. Before her thousand-yard stare pulled focus onto her son just a few feet away.

'Yeah, I'll be on the road by seven. Show starts at seven-thirty. Route planned out.'

The enormous barrel of Keelan's shotgun was halfway into the room before Erin saw it. The sight of the weapon pointed at her son made her scream. She had to be forgiven for that.

Brandon jumped.

Then spun ninety degrees to see his father aiming a Mossberg 12-gauge at his face.

'What the fuck?' yelled Brandon, as he fell backwards off his chair.

'I'm not going to let you do this, son,' said Keelan, keeping the gun tight on his little boy.

'Do what?'

'DON'T FUCK WITH ME, BRANDON,' Keelan roared, the abrupt volume change prompting another piercing scream from Mrs. Clark as she stumbled back against the kitchen units. 'I don't know how that all just came out, but we heard every word. You're going to kill kids today. That's what you're planning. You fucking animal.'

Brandon's eyes searched the air, as he tried to piece together how this had happened.

'No, I'm not,' Brandon answered like a child... but then his thoughts trumped his denial, *'How the fuck do you know? I didn't say it out loud.* Were you reading my texts?'

'I didn't have to. I heard you say it. We heard you say it.'

Brandon glanced at his mum. Her features were so twisted by shock, he almost didn't recognise her.

'You've got guns in your car. And I ain't gonna let you out of this house to get 'em. I'm not going to be that parent on the fucking news that says they never saw it coming, while everyone blames them anyway,' Keelan said, shaking like an addict going cold turkey.

Incredibly, Brandon took a deep breath, picked himself up from the floor, straightened his T-shirt and met his father's gaze.

'You ain't gonna use that. Not on me. I'm your kid. You're my dad. You ain't gonna shoot your boy, are you?'

Keelan loosened his hands before gripping his gun tighter, inching it closer to Brandon's chest.

'Shoot you, or let you shoot a load of kids, is that the choice you're giving me?'

'I ain't shooting any kids, dad. What the fuck are you on about? Get out of my way.'

And he was off. Side-stepping the muzzle and out into the hall before taking the stairs two at a time.

Keelan was frozen. It took Erin's gentle hand on the gun to release his muscles enough to lower it.

'You heard it, didn't you, Erin? It wasn't just me, was it?'

'No, it wasn't just you, Keelan. I heard it. I heard it all.'

Keelan Clark rested the shotgun against the wall and put his arms around his wife. She squeezed him harder than she'd ever squeezed him before. And just for a moment, Keelan surrendered to it.

Until a thumping of heavy boots coming from the upstairs landing broke them apart. Keelan marched into the hallway to see his son bounding down the stairs, now dressed in black and wearing an ammo vest.

'Son, you're not-'

Three huge bangs later and Keelan was gurgling on the floor with two holes in his chest and thick crimson gushing from a neck that had been ripped open by the third bullet.

Brandon was dressed for the day and clutching the Smith & Wesson 9mm handgun he'd also bought last week from the same store. It had been on special offer, at only $359.99.

He met his mother in the kitchen doorway, raised the gun again and put one into the top of her left cheek, watching the shape of her head wobble and change as the round tumbled through and out the back of her skull.

He took off. That wasn't planned. But fuck it. He was dying today anyway.

What was even more extraordinary about what happened next was that, even after her terrible injuries, in one of those strange examples of superhuman strength most likely caused by a primeval urge to do something important before collapsing, Erin managed to crawl to her neighbour, raise the alarm and give a description of her son's car before falling unconscious, being taken to hospital and put into a medically induced coma.

What Brandon couldn't have foreseen was that most of Boston's schools would quickly message parents to keep their kids at home that day until they could figure out what was going on with all the thinking out loud business.

So, an hour after he left the house, without getting anywhere near a school bus, Brandon's entire body was perforated by a wall of gunfire on the outskirts of the city after a televised car chase... that also happened to be live streamed on Rollo.

And Erin?

Well, after a few weeks, she came round to the news of her son's spectacular death... and that her best friend in the whole world... hadn't made it.

Erin Clark wished she'd never woken up.

Heavy shit, right? Pure, unadulterated honesty was wreaking havoc anywhere there were people.

3:11 am.
California.

In West Oakland, across the bay from San Francisco, after Jamal Harris had woken Ella Harris with the point of his dick that was standing up and twitching like an excited baby's arm... while Jamal was taking Ella roughly from behind... they were both caught having out-loud fantasies about their mutual friend Tom. Ella pretending it was Tom's cock penetrating her even more deeply than Jamal's and Jamal imagining Tom moaning back at him, his face loaded with ecstatic pain, in the mirrored door of their bedroom closet.

The divorce wasn't pretty, but at least it was quick.

12:11 pm.
Munich.

Sabine Schneider's journalistic career had been nothing short of stella. It had taken her to war zones all over the world. But after Syria, when bits of her cameraman had been blown through a wall and she'd lost half her right hand, Sabine had grown tired of boarding military transport planes in the dead of night. The letters she had to leave for her family, to be opened if she never came home, had become impossible to write. She needed something far less sketchy, where there were no bombs exploding and shrapnel flying.

So, after she'd got a call to front a new lunchtime show on Germany's most popular TV channel, "giving women an influential platform to discuss the big issues that women-of-today are facing", as the sales pitch went, she figured "Why not?". Maybe she could use her experience, of conquering fear for a higher purpose, to inspire a new generation of girls that there was nothing stopping them from going out there and changing the world.

She would be presenting the light entertainment programme "Frauen Power!" The show that, according to the theme tune, "empowered women everywhere" (as long as they lived in Germany or Austria, where it was broadcast).

So, it was a damn shame that, after The Event happened while she was live on air, Sabine Schneider would be remembered, not for the more virtuous, courageous chapters of her once dazzling career, but for what happened next.

At 12:11 pm, she was mid-interview with Bibi, the beauty vlogger from Stuttgart.

Sabine's frustrated, fuming thoughts that were broadcast to the show's entire seven-million-strong viewership, were how sickening it was, that a talentless little cunt like Bibi could be earning over twice as much as her, for showing children how to apply a bit of lippy.

10:11 am.
Burkina Faso.

And then there was Imani Mohamed Abdikadir, a Boko Haram fighter shooting the breeze over a breakfast of brouille, sitting around the last embers of their campfire in W du Burkina Faso National Park, with his fellow jihadis: Ahmed and Jibari.

They were debating how best to co-ordinate a multiple child "suicide" bombing attack on French forces across the Nigerian border, when 10:11 am came around.

At that precise moment, feeling a little morning glory rising in his combats, poor old Imani wasn't thinking about gloriously murdering a bunch of infidel soldiers.

He was daydreaming about planting a long, lingering kiss on Jibari's lips, running his fingers through his beard and imagining their tongues intertwining while his hand tickled down Jibari's ripped body to unbutton his camo trousers.

After that, it was fair to say, the day didn't go too well for him.

SIX

The Wake

An hour after The Event.
Somewhere in Essex.

Having finally noticed Doris drooped in her chair, Eddie had argued with Susie about the quickest way to get her to hospital. Susie had wanted to call an ambulance. Eddie suspected that would take too long and had eventually managed to cut through the layers of opinions coming from pretty much everyone there, to persuade his sister-in-law to drive the old dear to the nearest A&E.

Then, apart from the funeral director's mob and the two lads that Eddie had told to stay to look after the priest, everyone had retreated to their cars and had sat with their windows closed, stealing some much-needed privacy, speculating about what was going on and debating what the hell to do next.

Besides, no one wanted to leave before Eddie, just in case they decided against going to the wake and he caught them heading in the wrong direction.

Cars, tightly packed with black dresses and black ties, suffocating in perfume, were also filled with an intoxicating bemusement - and delight. Some people got it quicker than others. The ones that got it started playing with it, throwing outrageous thoughts back and forth, revelling in it as if it was a new superpower. Like synchronised automatons, most of them took to their phones, scanning their feeds to see if what was happening to them was happening to anyone else. The social world was indeed lighting up.

Once Eddie had finally driven off, the other cars peeled away and respectfully followed the snaking route out of the cemetery. Then some went left. Some went right. Jamie knew exactly which direction to go in.

'We're going,' said Jamie, following it up with an overlapping thought, *'we just fucking are.'*

'Yeah, well you're not driving, are you?' Georgie cut in from behind the wheel. 'Have you seen the state you're in? Your nose is all over your shirt.'

Jamie had his head back as far as his neck would stretch, trying to stem the bleeding, tentatively, painfully trying to reassemble his bone structure with the tips of his fingers.

'We've got to show our faces, Georgie… cuuuunt… even if mine's as bent as a fuuuuuucking nine-bob note.'

Georgie knew it was a pointless protest.

They'd been late, for starters. Then there was the weird shit by the graveside that they both knew could come back to bite them on the arse at any point, given a change of wind in Eddie's direction.

Over the years, Jamie had manoeuvred his way into Eddie's trust well enough to have tardiness forgiven. But disrespecting his dead missus? Fuck knows what Jamie had coming for that. If they didn't turn up to the wake, well, that would definitely be both feet well and truly over the line. And, when it came to Eddie Cox, everyone knew what that meant.

They had to be there and that was that.

'What are you fucking looking at?' thought Susie, keeping her eyes on the road while she felt her mother's glassy stare nagging at the side of her head. 'It's alright, mum,' she said to the windscreen and then to the rear-view mirror, 'we'll be there soon.'

There'd been a moment or two at the cemetery, where Susie could have sworn she'd been able to hear what Eddie and the others had been thinking. She'd heard them speak without opening their mouths, hadn't she?

'Nah. No fucking way. Shut up, Susie, you fucking moron.'

Susie's inner voice was always brutal with her. Today though, it seemed a lot louder. Clearer, more upfront in her head, the extra volume making it feel even more aggressive than usual.

Nope. Hearing other people's thoughts was not happening.

It'd all been pretty heated back there and, in truth, given the speed at which Eddie had shut her down and stuffed her and Doris into her car… she wasn't really sure what she'd heard.

'I need to back off the Citalopram,' she concluded, suddenly worried that maybe doubling

her prescribed dosage of antidepressants overnight, wasn't such a good idea after all.

The garbled, bubbling noises her mother was making weren't helping her get her mind straight either.

'What's that, mummy dearest?' Susie's out-loud-thinking was musical and spiked with venom. *'Can't you talk? Makes a change, dunnit?*

'You never could keep it to yourself, could you? All the hatred you felt for me. The love you showed Julie. It was always my fault, wasn't it? Your ugly daughter and the pretty one. Wasn't that how you introduced us once? I was old enough to understand, you fucking twisted bitch.

'Made all your mistakes on me, didn't you? Then tried to make up for it with Julie, putting her on that unreachable pedestal and putting me down every chance you could fucking get.'

Susie's flow was only interrupted by the occasional, shaky attempt at a comforting smile that she sent Doris' way.

Her mother, of course, could hear every word, which made these moments of disingenuous punctuation hideously sinister. The sweeter Susie tried to look, the darker it appeared. And Doris' face fell further each time.

'D'you remember sending me to my room without dinner for "cutting the cheese too loudly"? Cutting the cheese too loudly. Fucking hell. How is that even a thing?'

The last sentence slipped out of her mouth like temporary Tourette's.

'Remember that? You probably don't. Did you ever wonder what happened to your collection of canes? You know, the ones you used on me, what, every day, near enough? I fucking torched them. I took 'em to the woods and I fucking destroyed them. Then I burnt my foot on the ashes trying to stomp them into the ground. You even had a go at me about that, didn't you? Didn't occur to you to ask me how I'd done it.

'Fucking hell. I remember the expression on your face every time I did... well... anything. You looked like you were chewing a live wasp. I didn't just disappoint you though, did I? I fucking clawed through your skin...'

Susie rolled up to the back of a traffic jam and focused all her concentration on gently bringing the car to a stop… before snapping the handbrake up so hard it almost came off in her hand.

'… Didn't I? Claw through your skin?'

Susie looked at her mother square in the face. This time she couldn't bring herself to get anywhere near a smile.

'You hated the fact that I was there. That I was here. That I fucking existed.'

Transfixed by the pain pouring out of her daughter, Doris' pleading, creamy blue eyes started leaking badly.

But then Susie broke the spell and took in the streets around them, 'What the fuck's going on with the traffic?'

They were about a quarter of a mile away from the hospital now and it seemed like every car on earth was headed for the same place.

She checked the time on her dash. It'd been, what, just over an hour since Doris had started her stroke?

'Do you start a stroke?'

If that's what this was.

She looked at the sat nav.

Red streets.

Everywhere.

Not even orange.

Red.

It was a car park in every direction.

They weren't moving any time soon.

'Might be quicker to get out and drag you there. What do you think, Doris?'

Then she remembered an advert she'd seen on TV about strokes, where a hole burned into a man's head while he was watching football.

'Act fast, it'd said. Fast. F. A. S. T. The letters stood for something.. '

She played back the ad in her head.

'F was for Face.'

She studied Doris' now very asymmetrical clock, *'Yep, face... tick.*

'A. Arms. Arms limp? Yep.

'S. Speech, was it? Yeah, speech. Tick, that had gone.

'T... T... what was T for? Time? Was it time? Dunno. Wasn't a very good advert then, was it, if I can't remember what the acronym stood for? What else did it say, though?

'Act fast... "the faster you act, the more of the person you save" ... that was it!'

Just like she'd been taught when she felt a panic attack coming on, Susie slowed her breathing. She tapped the Spotify icon on her phone screen and surprised herself at how quickly her mind worked when she felt more relaxed. She knew exactly which tune she wanted to hear.

'I'm in the mood for a bit of Irma Thomas,' she thought out loud. *'You like her, don't you mum?'*

Susie turned up the volume, sat back in her seat and rested her soul as she sang along to Irma's rich, velvety tones.

'Ti-iiiii-iii-ime… is on my side… yes, it is.'

In a Range Rover, you were a cunt. Either a posh twat with more money than sense… or a gangster… with more money than sense.

But in a Land Rover, people let you out. They weren't even that bothered if you cut in front of them. A Land Rover was more "farmer". And these days, they had all the luxury of a Cuntmobile but without the "Key-Me-I'm-A-Cock" or "Pull-Me-Over-And-Search-My-Boot" factory-fitted bumper stickers.

Eddie Cox was as wild as the tundra, but he'd chosen his car very carefully. Like he made most of his business decisions. It was this rare combination of aggression and awareness that had carried him to the top of his little tree in the forest. Of course, to

Eddie and to most of the drug trade in his county, it was a mighty oak.

He'd grown up working for Jimmy Lynch, a man with a fiercer reputation than Eddie had eventually learned was warranted. A mythical big fish in a very tiny pond, as it turned out.

Eddie had cut his teeth down at Tilbury Docks, running vanloads of smuggled cigarettes as far west as Whitechapel and as far as they could in the other direction, all the way to Southend. At the time, it felt more like an ocean than a pond. But, like going back to your first school as an adult, everything seems so small through grown up eyes. In the end, complacency (and a lack of ambition) got Lynchy and a few others banged up.

Five years.

For fags and tobacco, for fuck's sake.

The risk wasn't worth the effort.

Eddie had no trouble filling the void, quickly turning his attention to cargo with a much more lucrative margin. Pills first, Ket and MDMA powder later, with a little home-grown cannabis on the side. Now it was almost exclusively cocaine. It was simpler that way. He'd settled on a great source in Dubai, put Jamie in charge of distribution, as well as making sure the cash flowed back to the Middle East, and business expanded fast.

But then the Albanians came and it all started getting out of hand. The "Hellbanians" were just wired differently. They gave even less of a fuck than Eddie's firm. And it took all his patience and diplomacy to broker a deal, using Dubai as leverage.

Albania was conveniently positioned at the halfway point, so he brought them in on his supply chain. The system the Hellbanians had worked out to control the containers coming into Tilbury was a thing of beauty. Just outside the port of Durrës, they converted the insides to look like offices, clubs, garages, brothels and even torture chambers, listing the containers as film sets. The more unusual the contents, the more plausible it was, so stashing the gear in amongst it all was lemon fucking squeezy.

It was a perfect partnership.

Luckily, they knew it.

They'd have the run of the Grays - Barking – Romford triangle, while he turned north from Basildon up to the insatiable middle-class appetites of Chelmsford and Colchester. His organisation had grown plump on the proceeds. And Jamie was a solid right hand.

So, an hour after The Event, it was in the cocooned tranquillity of his Land Rover Discovery, that Eddie found himself alone with his thoughts.

Time he'd normally relish.

Today it was excruciating.

Heading home, leaving Julie to the worms.

'All this money. All this success. And excess. A huge house. With no voices to fill it. No kids. No wife. No one to trust. Jamie and the rest? They're not friends, they're employees. And every one of 'em wants the top spot.

'Jamie. Of all people. Fucking cheeky slag. Beyond out of order. But it was weird the way it happened. Like… like he didn't really say it. But I heard it. I heard it. Actually, it wasn't just me that heard it, was it? It was his voice. But the words didn't come from his mouth.

'Or did they? Fuck me, it's foggy. Is it the red mist? Is it the grief? And this voice… I'm aware of it. I've never thought about it before… It's my voice. It's still inside my head… but it's different. I can hear it more. It's right up front. At the top of my brain. And it's fucking loud.

'I think I'm overloaded. Stay busy, Eddie. Stay busy. One foot in front of the other. As fucking hard as that is. Check in with the caterers. That's next. You'll deal with the Jamie thing later.'

Eddie pressed a button on the steering wheel and spoke to the car.

'Call Yolanda.'

The ring tone seemed to last a while. It took so long for his call to be answered that when it did, he immediately asked, 'Yolanda? What's wrong?'

'Nothing's wrong, Mr. Cox. Nope, it's all fine. We're all set.'

In the background, Eddie could hear shouting, arguments, crockery smashing. Yolanda barked an order with the phone away from her mouth before coming back and recomposing herself, 'It's all in hand. We're good. What time d'you think you'll be here?'

'I'm five minutes away,' Eddie said. 'And the guests won't be long either. Yolanda…'

'Yes, Mr. Cox.'

'Honestly, is everything really OK? Have you… erm… has anything… strange happened?'

'Strange? No. Nothing strange. The food's cooked and we're plating it all now. Everything's fine.'

'OK, good. Don't let me down, Yolanda.'

'I won't, Mr Co-'

Eddie hung up.

He used that phrase a lot. "Don't let me down" were just the right words in the right order at the right time to get someone to put in that little bit more effort, to go above and beyond. It started working for him when he'd risen high enough for it to carry a deeper, more loaded meaning.

'I'm delling you. I don't pucking know how, but he heard what I was dinking. I mide as well have said it oud loud.'

Jamie had a rolled-up tissue wedged in each nostril.

'Can you hear yourself?' Georgie said. 'Are you saying he's telepathic or something? *Shit, the lights are going red.*'

Georgie pumped the brakes, repeatedly whacking Jamie's head against his headrest until his fingers slipped and pressed hard into the bridge of his busted schnozz.

'JESUS PUCK, GEORGIE! No, not just Eddie. All of us. I can hear what you're dinking right dow.'

'Shut the fuck up, Jamie, that's insane. I'm more interested in what you said about Julie. Where the fuck did that come from? Did you fancy her that much? *OK, green. First gear, eyes up. Watch this car coming out of the side turn.*'

'No. I didn't fancy her. She was fit, yeah, but she was the boss' missus, for fuck's sake.'

'The boss' missus. That was the only thing stopping you, was it? That's not the answer I was looking for, Jamie.'

'It was a fucking crazy thing to be thinking, I get that. But don't tell me you've never had weird, inappropriate shit pop into your head at a funeral.'

Georgie thought about it.

'I suppose… there was that time at my uncle's cremation… when I sang the Countdown theme tune in my head, while the coffin rolled into the furnace. I timed it perfectly as well… bada bada badadada BING, just as the doors closed on him.'

But then, when she finally spoke, what came out was, 'No, I haven't. I'm not as warped as you, Jamie.'

Jamie carefully retrieved the bullet-shaped, blood-capped tissues from his nose.

'You're fucking lying, Georgie. I know you are because I just heard what you were thinking.'

'Oh yeah? What was I thinking then? *Shit, I'm in the wrong lane. I wanna go left, sorry mister. Indicate. I need to move over, thank you, sorry!*'

Jamie breathed the sigh of a man about to win an argument.

'Your uncle's cremation. Singing the theme to Countdown.'

'That's not in the same fucking league as what you said. Wait. Shut up. Nah, I must have said that out loud.'

'You didn't say it... you thought it,' thought Jamie, compelled to keep testing it, to make sure it wasn't just him going out of his tiny mind.

'Shit, I didn't see your lips move. How are you doing that? Do it again.'

Overtaken by curiosity, Georgie took her eyes off the road to watch Jamie's face intently. 'Do it again while I can see your mouth.'

'There's a woman with a push chair on the zebra crossing,' thought Jamie.

'Fucking hell, Jamie - what the fuck? I can hear what you're thinking!'

'Good, coz there's a woman – WITH A PUSH CHAIR - ON THE ZEBRA CROSSING!'

Georgie watched Jamie press his hands hard into the roof of the car before she turned to see that there was, indeed, a woman with a small child in the middle of the road, wide-eyed and frozen rigid.

'Shiiiit. I'm going too fast. I'll never stop in time. Fuck, fuck, fuck!'

Georgie's feet slammed on as many pedals as they could find, while her arms yanked at the steering, flinging the car towards the kerb. The paintwork on the front wing kissed the woman's jeans as they went past, the near side wheel mounting the pavement before the brakes finally did what they were designed to do.

'Fuck, Jamie.'

Then through the glass of her window to the enraged young mum, 'I'm so sorry.'

'Find somewhere to stop,' said Jamie. 'We need to get this worked out before we get to Eddie's.'

And that's how Jamie and Georgie found themselves in a Lidl car park, knowing that neither of them had to open their mouths to have a conversation.

'OK. How are we going to deal with this?' Georgie thought, at a complete loss herself, desperately hoping Jamie had a plan. *'This is a massive problem.'*

'Yeah, I know. You don't need to tell me how big the fucking problem is. Heaping the pressure on ourselves isn't gonna help us solve it, is it? Do you think I want Eddie Cox inside my head?'

'No, you don't understand, Jamie. There's… there's something you don't know.'

'What? What don't I know, Georgie? I would say that right now would be a good time to give me all the fucking information I need, to try and get us out of this fucking mess-'

Georgie's thought popped into her head before she had a chance to time her delivery, *'Julie was seeing someone else behind Eddie's back.'*

Physically, Jamie stopped statue still. But his mind continued to race, processing the news by repeating it.

'Julie was seeing someone else… behind Eddie's back. OK. And you know this… how?'

'She told me.'

'When?'

Georgie switched back to speaking her words. She could cope with hearing the odd thought coming from Jamie's head but conducting and following an entire conversation was confusing. She found that trying to exchange words in the right order, just in her mind, took a lot of effort and it meant that she wasn't thinking naturally anymore.

'A few months ago. On a night out. Does it matter when?'

Jamie pursed his lips and blew, *'Well, I suppose if it was recent... if she told you on her death bed or something... then it might be relevant. But no, actually, I don't suppose it does matter. Who was it?'*

'She was really unhappy, Jamie. Eddie was never around.'

'Who was it?' Jamie insisted, automatically matching Georgie's switch back to speech.

'D'you remember Ricky?' said Georgie, her chest dropping as she exhaled, like she was exorcising a demon, the pressure valve finally coming off.

'Ricky? Ricky who?'

'Sarah's fella.'

'Sarah?'

'Fucking hell, Jamie. You've got a memory like a sieve. Are you ever actually in the room when we go out with people? Sarah and Ricky. You've met Sarah a few times. I used to work with her at that advertising agency. Ricky came out with us once. That's when he met Julie. Fuck. I introduced them. Fuck.'

'I remember important shit, Georgie. Memorising the names of your mates isn't high up on my list. I've got enough to think about as it is.'

'Oh, whatever. The fact is, I know about it and Eddie doesn't. What if I think about it while we're at his place?'

'Well, what's the problem? Ricky'll be in the shit, won't he? He's got it coming if he's fucking around with a drug dealer's wife.'

'Yep. Ricky'll be in the shit, alright. But so will I. And if Eddie knows I know, then he'll assume you knew too and didn't tell him.'

'Fuckin' 'ell.'

'Yeah, fuckin' 'ell.'

'Hmmm… well, look, we don't know if Eddie's worked out this thinking out loud thing yet. And if he hasn't, we're not going to be the ones to tell him.

You're just gonna have to not think about it while we're there.'

'That's brilliant, Jamie. Genius. Have you ever tried to NOT think of something? Let's try that, shall we? Don't think of an elephant.'

'Elephant.'

'See?'

Georgie tilted her head back and rubbed her face, forgetting about the thick make up she'd carefully applied that morning.

'OK. What do we do?' thought Jamie.

'What can we do?' thought Georgie.

'Shut up, I'm trying to think.'

'You shut up. I'm trying to think as well.'

'Great,' thought Jamie. *'Solving a problem by working through it yourself, logically, without stupid interruptions… that's clearly gone out the window… hasn't it?...* Out the window… mmm… OK, let's test this.'

'What d'you mean?'

'See if you can hear what I'm thinking when I'm outside.'

Jamie pulled the door handle, stepped out of the car and walked round to Georgie's side.

'Can you hear me know?'

'Yes, I can hear you,' said Georgie through the glass.

Jamie took a few steps back.

'What about now?'

'Yep. I can still hear you.'

This time, Jamie retreated to a few parking spaces away.

'Are you thinking something?' Georgie said.

'WHAT?' Jamie called back.

Georgie pressed the button to lower the window, 'WERE YOU THINKING SOMETHING JUST THEN?'

'YES, I WAS,' Jamie shouted.

A smile crept across his face as he walked back to the car.

'I couldn't hear it,' Georgie said as he got in. 'What were you thinking?'

'I was thinking what a shit driver you are. Come on, let's go. *We might just be able to pull this off.'*

Georgie turned into the dusty country lane that served a handful of palatial houses on the outskirts of Billericay, an ancient settlement dating back to the bronze age and now a sleepy commuter town where, apart from a one-off scandal about a paedo politician and the odd raging drunk pissing up the Georgian Grade II listed wall of the library, nothing ever happened. No unwelcome attention. Just how Eddie needed it.

'Remember, it's all about distance,' said Jamie as they approached the last house on the left. 'I don't know exactly what the cut-off point is, but we need to get ourselves away from him as soon as we can. Thank Christ the rain's holding off. We can fuck off out to the pool after we've done the necessaries.'

'It's the necessaries I'm worried about, Jamie. How do I stop myself thinking about Ricky? Right now, it's the only thing in my head.'

'Yeah, I can imagine. OK… so, you need to be thinking about something else while we're talking to him. You need something to concentrate on, so it doesn't just pop in there.'

'Like what?'

'I saw this thing on TV once. It was a show where they had to memorise long lists of stuff. They got trained how to do it. And the trick was to tie the objects together in your mind by making up visual stories about them. The weirder the story, the more surreal the images were, the more they remembered.'

'OK, and?'

'Well, what about if you try to remember something that happened to you that was fucked up... or funny? And then keep that in your mind when you're around him.'

'That's just great, Jamie. He's gonna think I'm fucking nuts. Or rude. Or both. It's Julie's wake for fuck's sake. Why would I be thinking about something messed up or funny?'

Jamie shrugged.

'So, what do you want to do then? You got a better idea? Whatever it is you're thinking of, it ain't gonna be as bad as Julie fucking Ricky, is it?'

'That's true. OK, you've made your point. *And I can't think of anything else, so...* shit, I need something quick, Jamie, we're here.'

'Bollocks,' Jamie whispered.

'What?'

'Well, look around. There aren't many cars here, are there? *Fuck it, maybe there's enough. There's probably more to come. The more distractions for Eddie to have to work his way around, the better. It'll be alright, Jamie, you've got this. You gonna have to have fucking got this.'*

'You talk to yourself? I mean, like really talk to yourself. Use your own name and everything.

Fucking hell,' Georgie said as she curled the car into an empty spot on the vast gravel driveway.

'Fuck off,' Jamie said sideways.

In spite of it all, Georgie chuckled. It was just enough of a moment to release her brain from the grip of stress, so a memory could make its way to the front.

'I've fucking got it,' she said. 'Remember our second date?'

'What?' Jamie snapped, still irritated by the piss take.

'You took me to the zoo.'

'Did I?'

'Yeah. D'you remember the thing with the chimpanzee?'

Jamie searched. Then his eyes lit up when he found it.

'Fuck, Georgie… yeah, that's perfect.'

Georgie smiled warmly and Jamie nodded coolly, as they were let in by the man-mountain Eddie had posted at his front door.

Inside, people were huddled in small groups, unnaturally distanced from each other, squeezed into the corners and up against the walls of the huge living space.

A skinny teen, swamped by his waistcoat, shuffled past with no colour in his lips, balancing a tray of drinks. Georgie grabbed two glasses of white wine, upsetting the weight distribution.

The lad panicked.

'Don't drop it. Don't fucking drop it, whatever you do.'

He just managed to regain the tray's centre of gravity before taking a deep breath and offering it around the edges of the room. Yolanda had called her kid in to help out, after half her staff had fucked off when the thinking out loud started.

They spotted Eddie at the back of the kitchen having a word with the caterer who looked like she was about to burst into tears. Then Eddie spotted them.

'Fuck. He looks even more pissed off,' Jamie said out of the corner of his mouth.

'Well, he has just buried his wife,' Georgie said.

Eddie poured half a pint of Hennessy Paradis into a heavy crystal tumbler and bowled into the middle of the floor.

'Can you all get some fucking food. It's not gonna eat itself, IS IT?'

Eddie's voice rose to a boom as he spoke. Then, to himself, he followed it up with, 'It's not all burnt. Some of it's cold.'

A couple of the big units didn't need telling twice and they piled in. The others gingerly made their way over to the gargantuan spread and started foraging around like spooked deer.

Then Eddie was on them.

'Alright Jamie? Georgie.'

Georgie rested a hand on Eddie's arm and gave it a rub.

'How you holding up?' she managed, surprising herself with her acting skills. But then she felt her mind shifting to the thought that shouldn't be thought, so she swiped it away sharpish, *'Remember the kid at the zoo, screaming at the chimp.'*

Eddie closed one eye and shook his head. His day was getting more fucked up by the minute.

'Chimp? What fucking chimp?' thought Eddie.

A few drops of blood fell from Jamie's nose as he tried to fill the awkwardness with words.

'Eddie, listen, I don't know what the fuck all that was back at the cemetery.'

Jamie was genuinely sorry.

A little out of fear, maybe, but more from the heart. He'd known Eddie and Julie a long time.

Even with the amount of cognac cursing through him, Eddie was perceptive enough to pick up on it and he softened a little.

'Forget it.'

'Nah, I'm sorr-'

'Just leave it,' insisted Eddie. *'For now. We'll leave it for now.* Anyway, you're bleeding all over my fucking rug. Georgie, can you help him out here?'

'The chimp shat in his hand and chucked it at the little kid. Hit him right in the face. What's that?' Georgie said eventually.

'Twinkle toes here. Your boyfriend. He's bleeding.'

Eddie extended an arm behind them and nodded towards the stairs.

'Go get him cleaned up. You know where the bathroom is.'

Grateful for the out but resisting the urge to bolt, Jamie and Georgie thanked Eddie before sliding away as casually as they could.

'And get yourself a proper drink,' Eddie called after Jamie. 'You white wine wanker.'

'Did you see all Julie's stuff?' Georgie said to Jamie as they stood by the pool. 'I can't believe she's not gonna need it anymore. That came out wrong. I meant...'

'I know what you meant.'

Jamie had nabbed a couple of beers and Georgie had put a splash of tonic into a large glass of vodka as they'd styled their way through the kitchen and out into the garden.

'Yeah,' Jamie sighed. 'This is gonna change things for us, Georgie. She was a good influence on him. Kept him stable. Kept his temper in check. He's sharp as nails and he makes all the right choices when it comes to business, but when things get personal... his default setting is... well... it's unpredictable at best.

'Did you hear what he was thinking when we got here? He's got me marked. Julie would've talked him round. Now he hasn't got her voice of reason in his ear, there's no one to stop him going off the rails.

'How am I gonna navigate through this? He's gonna have time on his hands now, isn't he?

Probably wanna get more involved again. Fucking hell, I was doing alright. Now I've got to operate with him breathing down my neck. And I'm already on the naughty step.

'*I've lost control of my future, haven't I? That's a fucking feeling, that is. The way my life goes? That's at my boss' whim now, like every other sad cunt out there. Great.*'

'You'll get there,' Georgie interrupted. 'You've got this far. You'll just keep going. I know you. You will. You'll get back on his good side. But right now, you're gonna have to snap out of it, 'coz he's coming over.'

'Not a very good turnout, is it?' said Eddie as he reached them, looking around at the smattering of bodies in the garden and back up at the house, before taking a long lug on a vape shaped like an American Second World War grenade.

'Well, I suppose with everything that's going on,' Georgie said, far too quickly.

Jamie shot her a look.

'What d'you mean?' Eddie asked, producing a sweet-smelling cloud of vanilla and apple, five times the size of his lungs.

'The zoo. The zoo. The kid winding up the chimp. The chimp throwing his shit,' thought Georgie, forcing the memory from the back to the front her mind.

'She alright?' Eddie said to Jamie.

Jamie came to the rescue.

'Yeah, she's alright. Well, not really. She's in a state about Julie. She saw all her things when we were upstairs.'

'Ye-eah, I dunno what I'm gonna do with all that,' said Eddie to some invisible point on the horizon. 'Anyway, take this,' he handed Jamie a smartphone. 'It's PGP modified. I've got us all on a new encrypted network – VIPe, it's called.'

Georgie was now really struggling to hold back the bad thought. It was pushing hard, trying to muscle its way out.

She focused everything on the other memory, *'The shit flew through the wire and smacked the kid right in the chops.'*

'It's supposed to be the best,' Eddie said with half an eye on Georgie. 'No chances taken. Complacency gets you nicked. Or worse, right?'

'Yeah, course. Good idea, thanks,' Jamie said, trousering the phone and widening his eyes at

Georgie who looked like she was about to get hit by a truck.

'The best bit was the soft lump of shit that flew straight into the kid's screaming mouth. That shut the little cunt up. He nearly choked to death.'

Georgie had her eyes closed tightly now, as though she was waiting for the impact.

'OK, enough's enough,' said Eddie. 'Georgie what the fuck are you talking about? What's the fucking deal with the chimp shit?' Eddie had finally lost patience with how surreal his world had become, *'This can't be the grief. Or the fucking brandy.'*

Jamie instinctively knew it was time to put his hands up.

'She's trying not to think about something, Eddie,' Jamie said. Even though he was adapting their plan on the fly, his stomach still dropped like it was in a lift after the cable had snapped.

This could go either way.

'Oh yeah? And what's she trying not to think about, Jamie?' Eddie sucked hard on his grenade.

Jamie looked up at Georgie, who was staring back at him, shaking her head, 'She was trying not to think about something Julie told her a while ago.'

'RIGHT, EVERYONE OUT! FUCKING OUT. NOW. THANKS FOR COMING, YEP. BUT YOU CAN ALL FUCK OFF NOW,' Eddie announced as he herded the entire gathering towards his front door. 'And your lot, Yolanda, yep. Don't worry about clearing up. Just fuck off. See ya later.'

There was confusion, of course, but everyone was just glad to be getting out of there. Yolanda's water main finally burst and Big Unit 2 grabbed a whole tray of cold, burnt sausages as he went.

Jamie and Georgie were last.

Jamie gallantly pressed Georgie out the front door ahead of him, waiting to take whatever hit was coming his way.

Eddie stood in the hallway with his eyes down. Jamie stopped to say something. Then couldn't think of anything that would help, so he walked on.

'Jamie,' Eddie's voice was quiet.

Jamie turned like a condemned man.

'I appreciate you telling me. That took balls, that did. And I get it: trying to protect your missus.'

Jamie nodded and took a step.

'But Jamie…'

'Yes, Eddie?'

'I need his address.'

'I know. I'll text you. It won't take long.'

'You're a good number one, Jamie.'

'Cheers mate,' Jamie said, finally feeling dismissed.

As his guests dissolved into the evening, Eddie reached into his pocket and pulled out a lump of coke the size of a cue ball.

'This wasn't how it was supposed to go.'

SEVEN

The Landing

An hour after The Event.
Stansted Airport.

The last half hour of flight FR603 from Gran Canaria to London Stansted had been surprisingly undramatic. Angie and Poppy had managed to get everyone back into their seats relatively easily. Most of the passengers had behaved themselves with the calmness that comes from the fear that something odd was happening on their flight while they were still in the air. And odd-on-a-plane – on your plane – is never a good thing.

Everyone wants their particular flight to be as uneventful as possible. Mishaps, mistakes and crashes happened to other people's flights, not yours.

So, when something does happen, people are generally more than willing to make things feel as orderly as possible. And, when you're helpless inside a fragile white tube travelling at five-hundred miles an hour, thirty-eight-thousand feet up, when you know your fate is completely in the hands of two pilots and magical machinery that's far too complicated for you to ever understand... following the rules, sitting down in your designated seat with your seat belt on, is the only thing you feel you can do to help prevent whatever the problem is, from getting worse.

So, that's what everyone did. Sat there, staring at the back of a trio of heads, listening to voices coming from every direction. The impossibility of the truth far too strange to contemplate being real. The only mouths people could see were the ones either side of them. So, many wrote off what was happening as everyone suddenly feeling the need to speak. That seemed far more plausible than any alternative.

There were a few though, who were a little more open-minded, who entertained the possibility that what was happening was thinking out loud. And just the fact that they considered it, allowed them to explore it with the person next to them. If that person was open to it, of course. If they weren't, then the stewardesses had another freak out to deal with. Which they did. Their demeanour shifting to that detached, protocol-following, machine-like professionalism that air crews seemed programmed to follow, as well as doctors emotionally distancing themselves from trauma.

And so, the spiritual and the creative among them had begun to work it out and have their suspicions confirmed. Though the realisation was no less frightening than not understanding at all.

When it came to her children, Sarah had resorted to the digital cosh, as she called it: screens and headphones. Once they were settled, she'd put her own noise-cancelling ear buds in without playing any music, using the miracle of technology to block out the voices, especially the sound of the old fart's grumbling. She kept a vigil on the back of Pat's cherry red head and her springs tightly coiled, fully expecting him to swing round at any moment and resume the fight.

But it never came.

In the end, as the adrenalin drained away, she felt a familiar, fetid desperation seep into every cell of her body. It was the same feeling she got after every exhausting holiday, usually starting when her ears popped for the first time, the signal that the plane had started to descend and was delivering her back to the grey reality of life in the rain, with two relentless young kids and a husband who was never there, even when he was.

This was it.

This was her life now.

And she hadn't seen it coming.

She didn't just used to have a job; she had a career. On the way up as an Account Executive at an ad agency in London. It was a nerve-wracking, lip-smacking, soul-quenching, motivating, smooth-talking, high-walking, fast livin', ever givin', cool fizzin' lifestyle. And fuck, did she miss it. She used to roll with the punches, as they say. Give as good as she got. Take it on the chin and dish it out with interest. Now she found herself bursting into tears when the lid of the salad spinner came off.

She'd met Rick at a research group. He was a Data Analyst, crunching numbers for brands and advertisers who didn't so much as breathe without consulting his charts first.

Subsequently, Rick's confidence matched his salary and she'd fallen hard for it. Looking back, it wasn't that long before he'd proposed.

Of course, she'd said yes.

Rick was the only one who'd ever asked.

They'd been partners in crime for a while. Prosecco, parties and pills. But then the first bump came along. A bump in their road as well as her belly. Rick said he wanted it as much as she did, but his actions told her something different. He'd retreated and then tried to escape, turning a recreational pastime into a habit, doing way more coke, even on school nights, leaving her to do all the heavy lifting the next day.

Then there was the fucking affair.

All that soul-searching and yacking, yadda-yadda, into the small hours. Blah fucking blah fucking excuse fucking insecurity fucking blah.

And then having Cal, in some crazed attempt to make it all go away and get back to… what, exactly?

They'd never been right since Gabby.

Why the fuck would he ever change?

And having another one?

Well, if he wasn't absent before, that really did make him check out. The isolation made her sick to the pit of her guts.

On the rare occasion the planets had aligned, when he'd stayed sober long enough and she'd managed to find a suitable babysitter, they'd gone out for dinner. It used to be that they'd share a joke watching older couples sitting through their entire evening without saying a word. And they'd vowed never to become them. But here they were.

She felt like that hiker who'd fallen into some remote ravine and got his hand stuck between the rocks, having to make that impossible decision to saw his own arm off with a pen knife to give himself a better chance of living.

Divorce was a pretty blunt instrument too, wasn't it? And, she imagined, no less painful.

Oh, and why not throw this into the mix? The kids were going to suffer even more as they got older because they'd take all this shit into their relationships, wouldn't they?

Poor cunts.

Sarah had then spent the rest of the descent staring out the window, wondering if it would really be that bad if the plane fell out of the sky there and then.

After initially switching to following a lost-comms route, the pilots had resumed clear communication with Air Traffic Control, who'd somehow managed to stop the out loud thoughts of each controller from triggering their microphones. It's quite something to witness what well-trained human beings are capable of, when they're backed into a corner and lives are at stake.

In the end, the landing had been remarkably routine.

The passengers had disembarked, while having to listen to what Poppy thought of each and every one of them, from behind her perfect smile, as they reached the door.

'Snob. Wanker. Lay off the biscuits, fatty. For everyone's sake, use deodorant next time. Do you piss everywhere BUT the toilet bowl, when you're at home?'

The crew had stayed behind on the aircraft for post-flight checks and the most interesting debrief of their careers, testing their theories and agreeing that thinking out loud was the improbable, but only explanation. All flights had been grounded until the system could work out how to cope with this new, rather exciting development. And Angie was straight on the phone to Lilly.

And so it was that Rick, Sarah, Gabby and Cal found themselves in the middle of that infuriating, elasticated cordon of Beelzebub, snaking up and down a hideously patterned carpet, shuffling for miles to gain an inch of distance here and there towards border control.

There'd been a moment of pure horror for Sarah as the wheels had hit the tarmac, when she'd glanced down to check the boys' battery levels and discovered that Cal's was almost out. So, she'd retrieved yet another portable charger from her well-stocked inventory and was now clutching it like a digital umbilical, while her baby was oblivious to the electrical nutrition being fed into his iPad.

Rick was still reeling from his final minutes on the flight, having to listen to the disgusted tuts and teeth-kissing of the woman next to him, clearly but inexplicably aimed in his direction. Luckily though, he didn't have to dwell on it for too long because Sarah had given him a new problem to solve.

She'd told him about her ruckus with Pat as soon as they'd hooked up in the long, extendable gangway thingy just outside the plane.

For the first time in a while, Rick and Sarah had plenty to talk about. They had a mutual enemy. And both of them were craning their necks to see where baldy was in the queue.

'There he is,' said Sarah, as she spotted a glossy pink, slightly hairy, head-sized snooker ball. 'Thank fuck. He's way ahead of us.'

But she hadn't accounted for the elasticated snake cordon that spun Pat and Joan around and soon had them approaching from the opposite direction. She could feel Rick tensing up. And she could hear him working through options for what to say when Pat and Joan came close enough that they couldn't be ignored.

If she'd had her eyes on Rick, rather than switching between Pat and her kids, she'd have noticed that Rick's mouth hadn't moved through any of it.

'Just leave it, Rick,' said Sarah. 'I dealt with it on the plane. It's done. He's old. You're not. And let's just remember where we are, shall we? This is passport control. What are you going to do, punch him?'

'No,' said Rick. 'But you ended up in a physical fight with the man. I can't just let that go, can I? It'd be weird if I didn't say something.'

'It wasn't a fight. He didn't touch me.'

'You know what I mean.'

'Well, if you'd have been sitting next to me, it probably wouldn't have got to that, would it?' Sarah emphasised would it so much that a little bit of spit came out on the t.

Pat had already decided to get the first word in, despite Joan's peaceful protests.

'Ah, the husband. Where were you when your kid kept hammering the back of my chair?'

'Doesn't matter where I was,' said Rick. 'You threatened my child.'

'I didn't say it. But yes, I thought about it. Not that I would ever hurt a kid. Which brings me to what's probably a more important point… I don't know what the hell's going on, but somehow your wife heard it. And the next thing I know I'm having what little hair I've got left, ripped out.'

'You must have said it,' said Rick.

'Nope. I might be old but I'm not senile. I never said it out loud. I thought it. So, maybe you can tell me how your wife knew what I was thinking?'

'I heard you say it,' said Sarah. 'Stop trying to confuse everyone.'

'I'm not,' said Pat. 'Tell me, be honest, did you hear any other voices on the plane, young lady?'

'Well, yes. It did get quite loud, all of a sudden.'

'And how do you explain that?' said Pat.

Sarah shrugged.

'I can't. Everyone was just talking more than usual. And anyway, I had these two to look after.'

'All I know is that something's going on that we don't understand,' said Pat. 'You were able to hear what I was thinking. And I'm fairly sure I could hear what you were thinking too.'

'Bullshit. That's a load of crap. You're just trying to deflect it all away from you,' Sarah turned away and gestured for Rick to do the same.

But Pat wasn't finished. He leant in towards Sarah, prompting Rick to step between them.

'Is it crap?' said Pat. 'OK, put it this way then… I had to listen to your whole sob story all the way down. Did you say all of that out loud?' Pat's eyes flickered towards Rick, 'If you hate him that much – and I don't blame you – just divorce him.'

'What the fuck does that mean?' said Rick, as the blood rushed to his fists. 'What the fuck is he talking about?'

But Pat and Joan were being pressured from behind to fill the five-yard gap that had opened up in front of them. So, they trundled on, the wind well and truly knocked out of Joan's sails by the probability that it wasn't just happening to her.

Angie speed-walked smoothly through the airport, mobile in one hand, elegantly pulling her carry-on with the other. Any uniform in an airport tends to draw attention but Angie, in her bright scarlet suit, with her frame and her gate, turned heads in waves.

'I'm so sorry, I'm going to be later than I thought,' Angie said into her phone. 'It was a really strange shift. Something weird happened. Are you OK? How are things at the hospital?'

'I'm fine, mum,' said Lilly. 'I'm with Sag. Something weird has happened here too. But I think I know what it is.'

'What? What's happened? What's wrong?'

'Well, nothing's wrong really. It's difficult to explain. I'll tell you all about it when you get here.'

'OK. But you're OK, are you?'

'Yes, mum, I'm fine. I got here no problem and Sag's looking after me.'

'OK, good. I'm just getting to my car. I'll see you soon.'

'OK, mum. Oh, and mum…'

'Yes baby?'

'Please be careful. Promise me you'll drive slowly, there's no rush. There's been a horrible accident in the car park here and Sag told me that a lot of hospitals have had a big spike of emergencies in the last hour or so. He said to tell you to be extra careful on the road.'

'Sag. He's so sweet, isn't he? And he's there with you now?'

'Yes, mum. He's a keeper, isn't he?'

The relief that her child was safe allowed her to laugh a little at Lilly's banter. 'I suppose he is, yes. OK, I'm at the car. I'll see you soon. Love you.'

'Love you, mum. Drive safely.'

Rick had piled his family's luggage into the boot of a cab and the four of them were now headed home.

Gabby and Cal couldn't believe their luck with how much screen time they were being allowed, so they stayed as quiet as they could. Little people are sharper than we give them credit for. They were both fully aware that their parents were engrossed in something serious and that lifting their head to interact with them could be the end of their stint in the colour-saturated digital worlds they'd found to immerse their imaginations in. Mum and dad had clearly forgotten about their usual time limits, so why risk reminding them?

Rick had placed the kids in the far back seats of the people carrier to give himself the best chance of talking to Sarah without interruption, something the two of them hadn't managed in years.

At baggage collection, they'd tested Pat's thinking-out-loud theory and each of them, to their own personal horror, had realised he'd been right.

They'd sacrificed individual privacy when they'd moved in together. Then, when the kids came along, their sex life was easily (and often) interrupted… so, the last corner of private space they had – their own minds – now even that would be on display for anyone to gawp at.

Hideous.

They'd started to wonder (out loud) how this was going to affect their conversation, but they'd discovered on the way to the taxi rank, that their exchanges weren't affected as much as they'd feared. Talking out loud meant you weren't thinking out loud simultaneously because the brain was too busy telling the mouth what to say to have any other thoughts creep in at the same time. So, the conversation since had been relatively normal.

Normal but spikey.

And the spikes had gotten sharper since they'd been in the cab.

Sarah, feeling the most exposed by Pat's observations, had been searching through her social feeds for an explanation, using it as a distraction from answering the question Rick kept asking.

'What did he mean by "sob story"?' asked Rick for the third time.

'It's happening to a lot of people,' said Sarah.

'OK, so it's happening to a lot of people and, yes, it's fucking weird. And we're going to work everything out when we get home. There'll be a news report or something, if it's happening to everyone. But, right now, I'd like to know what that old fuck meant by your sob story.'

With the acceptance of knowing it was now pointless trying to avoid the issue, Sarah just came out with it.

'I'm not happy, Rick. I can't remember the last time I was happy. I can't remember the last time we were happy.'

They'd fixed it so the kids couldn't interrupt, but they hadn't accounted for the cabbie. Before Rick could respond to Sarah's nauseating admission, a completely out of tune, flat-as-a-pancake, *'Laydeeee eeeen red,'* crowed loudly from the front seat.

Before he'd picked up their fare, their driver had watched Angie cross the road to the short-stay car park and, in his mind, had been singing Chris de Burgh's "end-of-disco-slow-dance-side-to-side-shuffle-cuddle-classic" ever since, with the ear, the accent and the mangled lyrics that came from being tone-deaf and born, bred and buttered in Istanbul.

'Eeeza daaancing wiv meeee, chick to chick,' filtered back through the headrests. And in any other time or universe, it would have had Rick and Sarah wetting themselves.

But not this time.

And not this universe.

'I had no idea you were feeling that bad,' said Rick. 'I thought we'd got over all the shit since… well, you know.'

'Since you fucked someone else?' Sarah wasn't going to let him get away with not saying it or hearing it.

'But we discussed all that. I thought we'd straightened it out. I told you the reasons why it happened.'

'Yes, you did. And you framed it like you couldn't help it. Like it wasn't your fault. Penises don't accidentally fall into vaginas, Rick. They're forced in there very deliberately. You knew exactly what you were doing. And what were the other reasons you gave me again? I'd "ballooned" after having Gabby? Let myself go? You felt excluded from the family? My fucking arse. You've never really wanted to be part of our family, have you? You're never there, for a start.'

It took every connection in Rick's brain not to roll his eyes at the prospect of yet another repeat performance of their particular tragedy. The last thing he wanted to do was throw more fuel onto a fire that was burning all over again.

It never really went out, though, did it?

It just reduced to an ember, glowing unseen under a pile of ash, waiting for the slightest combustible thing to fall onto it, so it could catch and ignite.

Rick turned to the window and felt too empty to find any pleasure in the rolling fields of crops and livestock. Instead, the weight of the guilt forced his head down to stare at the soulless blurred tarmac on the hard shoulder of the M11.

'I don't know how to tell her the real reasons for it all, without sounding like an immature little cunt. It's going to sound stupid. Shallow. Insecure. Childish. But… I got more respect at work than at home. When I spoke, people listened to me. I got praise for a pitch win or a presentation. I was useful. Needed.

'I felt like a spare part when Gabby was born. It was like nature had made them close and I was on the outside looking in. That's why I spent so much time at the office. If I'm being really honest with myself, it's why I was doing so much coke. I could escape on that stuff.

'But I was different on the gear. It wasn't really me, was it? I was all fucked up and depraved. Only ever thought about what that other me wanted there and then.

'A family that I didn't know how to be a part of, seemed like a foreign country where I didn't understand the culture... or speak the language. And Cal, well, that really did make me feel like a fifth wheel.

'So, the self-medicating and the need to run away just got out of hand. I didn't know how to be a dad and I didn't know how to ask her to help me. It was like I should've known and asking would have been... well... failure.

'Not something a man should do, is it? He should work shit like that out for himself. I couldn't ask the woman I married to help me be a man. She'd never look at me the same again.'

Rick had been so wound up in himself, he'd forgotten he was thinking out loud. He looked up to see that Sarah was looking at him differently. But not in the way he expected.

'... or dee eye-lites in your air that cut your eyes,' the timing of the line from the driver's seat was epic.

Was that the sparkle back in her eyes again? God, he missed the warmth and reassurance that gave him.

Rick's phone buzzed and broke the moment.

He frowned when he saw who the message was from. And, for a split-second thought about how he could turn the phone away from Sarah so he could read it privately. But this was exactly the wrong time to be hiding anything from her.

Sarah could sense the sudden fall in Rick's face. So, she was keener than ever to see the message that had just come through, that had caused that familiar draining of colour from his cheeks. The last time she'd seen that was when she'd confronted him about his WhatsApp exchanges with the "accidental vagina".

'You've got a message,' said Sarah, looking down her nose at Rick's phone screen.

'I know,' said Rick, like a man on the gallows being told he had to put his head in the noose for the execution to continue.

'Who's it from?'

'Georgie.'

This wasn't a name Sarah had expected to hear.

'Georgie? Why the fuck is my friend messaging you?'

'Dunno.'

'Oh, fuck off Rick. Show me the message. Shall we read it together?'

Rick tapped it open and read it.

'EDDIE KNOWS. And he knows where you live.'

'Eddie knows what, Rick? Who the fuck is Eddie? How does he know where we live and why THE FUCK – IS – THAT - A - PROBLEM?'

'I never will for-het the way you luck tooniggghhhhh.'

Fuck's sake.

What Rick would do to swap places with the tone-deaf Turkish cab driver right now.

EIGHT

The Crush

An hour after The Event.
Addenbrooke's Hospital, Cambridge.

As it turned out, someone in the car park had been in the wrong place at the wrong time. Sag and Lilly had arrived at the window to discover that a woman had been gruesomely pinned against a wall by a car that, judging by the angle, had somehow lost control. The driver was out with his head in his hands. A lady was silently screaming from the passenger side and they could just make out a child's legs kicking in distress on a booster seat in the back.

Sag had shot out of the room to check that the right people were aware of it and that someone had organised the fire service in case there was cutting to do. Lilly watched as staff rushed to help. As terrible as it was, it occurred to her that at least the poor woman was already at a hospital.

Sag eventually came back to find Lilly still engrossed in the action. As much as he wanted to join her, he felt a duty to keep a twelve-year-old from what could be a harrowing aftermath. It didn't look good at all.

'As interesting as that is to watch, Lilly, shall we talk about what's happening to us?' said Sag, glad there was a distraction even more fascinating than the drama unfolding outside.

'Sure,' Lilly said, coming back to the bed. 'Do you think that lady will be OK?'

'I don't know. Hard to say. I hope so.'

'She was really unlucky, wasn't she?'

'Yep. Life can be like that, can't it? Bad things happen to good people,' said Sag, fully aware of the irony in who he was saying this to. 'Anyway, talking about good people… you've always said you wanted to be a doctor when you grew up. So, let's start your training now, shall we? Give me your best prognosis on why we can hear other people's thoughts.'

'Oh, I think it's a bit too soon to be coming to any conclusions, Specialist Nurse. I think we'll be studying this for some time,' Lilly said, putting on her best, clipped medical professional's voice. 'We'll need test subjects, of course. Would you like to volunteer, Mr. Masih?'

'I'd be happy to donate my body and brain to medical science, doctor. What do I need to do?'

'I think we should start with some practice. I'd like to see if we can conduct a full conversation just with our minds. Are you happy for us to proceed?'

'I certainly am, doctor. I'm in your capable hands.'

'Excellent. Then let's begin.'

Cross-legged on the bed, Lilly wriggled herself comfortable, while Sag settled into the chair next to her.

'May I go first?' thought Lilly.

'Be my guest,' thought Sag, feeling a compulsion to communicate chivalry by nodding his head and lowering an eyebrow, like his face was bowing to royalty.

'You look really funny when you think out loud, Sag.'

'Do I?'

'Yeah. It looks like you're trying to act out your thought with your face.'

They were both doing it. Automatically exaggerating their expressions to accompany each thought, trying to enhance the tone and meaning of every sentence.

'Is that bad?' thought Sag.

'Actually no, I don't think it's bad. I suppose it's what we do when we speak, right? It just looks really funny when your mouth's not moving.'

Sag laughed.

'You're doing it too, you know?'

'I didn't know,' thought Lilly. *'Thank you for telling me. That's the first point to note for our research: A tendency to over-exaggerate facial expressions. And may I ask that the test subject sticks to thinking rather than speaking, please?'*

'Ah, yes, of course. Think, don't speak. Got it.'

'OK then,' thought Lilly. *'Do you think this is just a temporary symptom or something more permanent? Are we going to be like this forever or do you think it'll go away?'*

'I have no idea, Lilly. Would you like it to go away?'

'God no. Sag, this is amazing for me. I've struggled to breathe for as long as I can remember. If I can talk without using any of the air inside my lungs, it'll be so much easier. It IS so much easier. I love it already. I hope it doesn't go away.'

'OK then, let's hope it doesn't go away,' Sag was struggling to fight the natural inclination to speak the words out loud. Lilly playfully berated him with a look, so he concentrated extra hard and switched back to thought. *'Although I think this is going to cause a lot of problems for a lot of people.'*

'Why?' thought Lilly. *'Isn't this the best? It means no one can lie anymore. If you can hear what someone's thinking, then you'll know how they're really feeling. Everyone HAS to be honest – all the time.'*

'Yes, they will have to be, Lilly, you're right. And that sounds like a fantastic thing, but when you're an adult - sorry... *when you're an adult, there can be lots of reasons why you're not honest with other people. Some of those reasons can even come from a good place.* It might be that you care about someone - damn, this is actually really hard... *it might be that*

you care about someone so much that you don't tell them the truth because you think it might hurt them.'

'Well, that doesn't make any sense,' thought Lilly. *'The only people I can think of who wouldn't like being honest all the time, would be bad people. People with something to hide.'*

'That's true, yes,' thought Sag. *'Bad people would be found out pretty quickly. But a lot of good people have bad thoughts too. They just dismiss them as bad thoughts and never act on them. Which is partly what makes them good people. If every bad thought that a good person had, was out loud for everyone to hear, you might mistake them for a bad person.'*

Lilly's eyes drifted unfocused to an invisible spot in the middle of the room as she processed Sag's point.

'Hmmm… yes you might,' thought Lilly. *'But if you have a good heart and you're forced to wear it on your sleeve, then people will know you're a good person. They'd know the real you, wouldn't they? And if you did have a bad thought, I think people would know it wasn't that bad because it wouldn't happen very often and you wouldn't act on it. So, it would still be a good thing to be able to hear people's thoughts because, if everyone knew the real you and*

they still liked you, you'd know they were proper friends.'

Sag had to admit that the kid's logic was pretty flawless.

'You're right, Lilly,' he said out loud. 'God, it's taking me a while to get used to this… *Yes, it would be a great test of friendships, wouldn't it? But, what about this? Adults are a lot more frightened than kids about telling other people how they really feel.'*

'Why does that scare you more as you get older?' thought Lilly.

'I think it's because you learn that being honest with people can backfire on you. People can take advantage of you. You worry that, if you're too open with them, they'll have power over you. So, a lot of people put on an act. They try to look strong, especially when they feel weak.

'And then there's the fear that seems to grow as you get older, that you'll be embarrassed or hurt if you're honest about your feelings for someone and they don't feel the same way about you,' Sag was getting the hang of it now. *'Most people hide things to protect themselves, Lilly. A lot of us aren't even honest with ourselves.'*

'Do you worry about that?' Lilly probed.

'What, about being honest with myself?'

'No. Do you worry about telling someone how you really feel about them because you're scared they don't feel the same way about you?'

Sag straightened up in his chair. He shifted his position and tried his hardest to keep the next thought from entering his head. But, of course, the effort made him think of it instantly.

'Yes. I do worry about that.'

'And do I know the person you're worried about?' Lilly grinned.

Sag couldn't believe he was being psychologically outmanoeuvred by a twelve-year-old.

'Wow. You're good, Lilly. I'll give you that.'

The image of Angie, when he saw her last, pinged into his brain.

'It's my mum, isn't it?' thought Lilly.

Sag heaved a huge sigh, all his longing rising from the depths again, combining forces with the guilt of overstepping a professional boundary.

'Can you see what I'm thinking too?' asked Sag. 'Did you just see what I saw?'

'No. I didn't see anything, Sag. I've just known for a while, that's all.'

Sag was more than relieved. His inner voice might not be private anymore but at least his imagination was still his own.

'I can't think of anyone better to be exploring this with than you, Lilly... *apart from maybe one other person,*' Sag said/thought.

And they both smiled.

Just then, Lilly's mobile rang and she grabbed it quickly.

'It's mum,' then into the phone, 'Mum? Hi. Yes, I'm fine. Sag's with me.'

The roads were a mess. Angie's sat nav kept trying to get her off the motorway to reroute her around accidents, but she'd tried that once and it was just as bad on the A roads.

Back on the northbound side of the M11, a few of the cars that were still moving kept weaving outside their lanes. Angie worked out that the ones most likely to be unpredictable had more than one person in them. Made sense. If they'd discovered this thinking-out-loud thing at speed on a motorway... she could understand how that would be a bit of a distraction for the driver.

Another wall of traffic slowed her to a crawl.

Through her windscreen, she could see a pile up on the opposite carriageway. So, that was it: people on her side had been rubbernecking. She'd normally get all self-righteous about that but this time, she wanted to gawp as much as the rest of them because this was huge.

There were cars and trucks everywhere and some were facing the wrong way. As she got closer, she saw what was left of a hatchback crumpled to half its length and stuck under the back of a lorry. Holy fucking shit. No one could have survived that.

But now her side had ground to a halt.

Her blood froze as she just managed to catch her brake pedal before she hit the back of a Volvo.

God, that was close.

Split-second panic over.

Her blood started to thaw.

Time to think.

For Angie, that wasn't always welcome.

She'd had a very different experience to a lot of families dealing with CF. Lilly wasn't diagnosed until she was three, so the first few years of Lilly's life had been terrifying, as she tried to figure out what was wrong with her baby and not getting any real answers.

So, when Lilly was finally diagnosed, while Cystic Fibrosis was a terrible label to be sewn into her, there was also a feeling of relief that Angie at least had somewhere to start on improving her child's life. She could get treatments. At last, she was given opportunities to help Lilly be as healthy as she could be.

The emotional element of CF was probably the aspect of the disease that had the most impact on her. The feeling of being out of control, not being able to fix something that was wrong with her child. That cut to the core.

She couldn't think of anyone she knew, in real life anyway, who had to go through what she went through every single day, watching her child in pain or struggling to breathe or having to be the one to hold her down for a procedure… she couldn't do all that and not be weighed down with worry. And guilt. There wouldn't be anything in her if she didn't feel that.

Without any kind of support system outside of strangers on a forum or staff at the hospital, doing it alone, as a single mum, the stress of having to leave Lilly alone in the house overnight, which she knew she shouldn't do but sometimes, she just couldn't help… trying to keep the subsequent depression at bay was like pushing water uphill. Because it didn't matter how good any of the other moments in her life were, there were these key points within CF life, that absolutely ripped her apart.

Then there was that humiliating search for personal support. Angie wasn't short of admirers, but finding someone who wanted to take on even some of the responsibility for a sick child who was never going to get better, well, they fell away with the slightest breeze, didn't they?

Like brittle autumn leaves.

And what about her own health?

With all the hurdles she and Lilly had to face together, Angie knew that if she wasn't healthy, then she wouldn't be able to take care of Lilly.

Now and again, she indulged the thought that maybe sometimes she should refocus on her own wellbeing. After all, she was a role model for how Lilly should take care of herself and she had to be a beacon for both of them, no matter how thick the darkness got.

The last thing she'd read on yet another CF website was that, when she felt low, she really needed to talk about it with Lilly's primary care team.

Basically, that was Sag.

He'd been there for Lilly for years. He'd be a good person to talk to. But she wasn't sure how to even bring it up with him, without looking like she was drawing attention away from her daughter.

Her wellbeing?

In front of Lilly's?

No, that didn't sit well at all.

Finally, the traffic was flowing again, as Angie reached the outskirts of the city.

'Thank god. She's OK. They landed fine. And she's on her way,' puffed Lilly, the stress taking extra breath from her body.

'That's great news,' said Sag. 'I'm glad you told her to drive carefully. I've just been talking to some of the other nurses and they're saying most A&Es are already struggling.'

They didn't know it at the time but lunchtime pub brawls, accidents on the road and a huge rise in domestic violence callouts were already stretching police and the NHS beyond their limits.

'So, yeah… my mum's on her way here. Are you going to talk to her?'

'Of course, I'm going to talk to her.'

'No, you know what I mean. Are you going to talk to her about how you feel about her?'

Sag blew through his lips and rubbed his chin.

'I… I just know it's not appropriate, Lilly. I mean… I need to stay professional about it all. You're my patient.'

'I am. But she's not.'

'Yes, I know, technically you're right,' said Sag. 'But she's your mum. She's the mother of my patient. She's your carer. And the rules do say… clearly… that any form of sexual… let's say romantic behaviour between a nurse and a patient - or their carer - is a breach of boundaries. Believe me, I've checked. More than once, actually.' He shook his head. 'I'd be overstepping the mark, Lilly… I could lose my job.'

'Mmmm…' thought Lilly. *'You could lose your job. Yeah, you could… IF they found out. Do you think my mum would tell them?'*

'Who knows how she'd react? And I can't really take that chance,' said Sag, his voice breaking a little with the despair of feeling his best opportunity so far, slipping away.

'I understand, Sag. But remember what's happening. You're hearing me right now. So, you might not be able to help it when she gets here. I mean, this is SO weird... those rules you're talking about, they weren't written with this in mind, were they? No one can blame you for having thoughts about someone.'

Sag wandered to the window and looked down into the car park. He saw a fire engine, an ambulance and a tarpaulin covering the area where the victim would have been. A tarp was never good.

'No, sure. But it's what I do with those thoughts that I suppose they'd get me on.'

'Sag.'

Lilly thought his name with such a knowing, confident tone that Sag turned towards her with hope in his eyes that she'd figured out a loophole.

'I don't know how long I've got left.'

Sag immediately tried to jump in. Lilly didn't let him.

'No, it's OK. We both know the truth. I don't know, no one knows, how much life I've got left in me. The thing is... I might not have long but I'm

hoping my mum does. And she needs someone to be there for her when I'm gone. When there's a tomorrow for her, that starts without me,' Lilly had read a line like that in a poem she'd seen on Insta and it had stuck with her. *'These rules you're talking about… when you look at them from where I am… they're silly. They're made up. They're invisible. Don't let something you can't even see get in the way. I know you'd make her happy.'*

Sag turned back to the window, rubbing away the salty liquid that had coated his eyeballs. He stared at the tarpaulin covering a woman who couldn't have been older than forty.

Life. It was, indeed, cruelly short. You never knew when your time was up. And, if this thinking-out-loud thing was going to be the new normal, then… what the fuck? Why not let it happen?

Sag turned and looked at this tiny shell of a person sat cross-legged on a hospital bed; a human being who deserved more life than anyone he ever knew.

'Like I said before, Lilly… you never cease to amaze me.'

Angie's arrival was by a sudden flash of scarlet and sweat bursting through the door. She raced across the room and wrapped her daughter up so tightly, her arms seemed to go around her twice. Sag's smile couldn't have been wider.

Then there was the pawing and the checking and the kisses that made up the sequence of making sure her kid was OK.

'Thanks for staying with her, Sag,' said Angie, double taking a little at the rim light around Sag's head and shoulders caused by a rare glimpse of sun streaming through the clouds.

'No problem. We've had quite a time of it, haven't we Lilly?'

'You could say that Sag, yeah. Mum, that weird thing that's happened. We know what it is.'

'Lilly worked it out. And she did it quicker than anyone,' said Sag.

'I think I do too,' said Angie. 'But you go first.'

'We can hear what other people are thinking, mum.'

Angie jumped and giggled. What had seemed like a disaster on the plane felt joyous coming from her daughter. It felt like their personal connection had just got even closer.

'So, it is happening for everyone,' Angie looked at both of them in turn to watch for her thought being registered.

'Yep, it looks that way,' thought Sag.

Angie laughed again, delighted by getting a response.

'So, what does this mean for today's review, Sag?'

'Well, from what I'm being told, emergencies are off the charts, so a lot of us are being redeployed. As you can imagine, there's a fair amount of confusion going on here. So, the machine has kind of broken down for the moment. Who knows when we'll be back up and running again. So, I'd say for now, get yourself and Lilly home safely and I'll be in touch when I know more about when we can get you both back in.'

Lilly frowned at Sag so hard, it looked painful. Sag's shoulders dropped and then shrugged.

'What can I do?' he thought, as Lilly's eyes tried to connect him to Angie by an invisible tether.

Angie read Sag's thought as a conclusion to his plan, 'I don't suppose there is anything you can do. Although, Sag…'

'Yes, Angie?'

'Now that Lilly's review is postponed… would you have any time for me?'

Sag looked at Lilly. Lilly looked at Sag.

'Err… sure. Of course I've got time for you. I'll find us somewhere we can talk.'

Sag walked towards the door, slowly at first, watching Lilly's eyes get wider and her eyebrows higher. Then he couldn't help himself and, as he left, he picked up the pace.

'What do you want to talk to Sag about, mum?'

'I just want to make sure I'm fit and healthy enough to look after you properly, that's all. Nothing bad. God, this whole having a conversation with your mind takes a bit of getting used to, doesn't it?'

'You'll get the hang of it,' thought Lilly, glad her mum couldn't see the image of tightly crossed emoji fingers she'd just conjured up in her brain.

Sag walked Angie down the hall to a spare room, their thoughts about what they were going to discuss overlapping each other's into a blur of words. They had a laugh about it as Sag opened the door and offered Angie a choice of chairs.

'Thanks Sag,' Angie began. 'Erm… I err… just wanted to talk to someone about… me, really.'

'Go on.'

'Well, I'm on my own with Lilly. I can talk to people online and that, but it's a little bit superficial. I don't get to the stuff that's… well… causing me to feel down a lot of the time.'

'OK. So, can I just say that I think you cover that very well when you're around Lilly. Does she have any idea about how you're feeling?'

'No, no. I tend to keep that from her, you know. I don't want her to feel bad about making me feel bad. She can't help her situation. So, yeah, I keep it as positive as I can when I'm with her.'

'You're such a strong person, Angie,' thought Sag. The tone of his thought deeply personal and heartfelt.

It took Angie by surprise and her mind staggered a little from the hit.

'I just… I just feel so drained half the time. I read somewhere that if I felt that way, I should talk to Lilly's care team.'

'Well, of course you can talk to us. *You can talk to me.* That's what we're here for.'

Sag was trying to keep the conversation in normal spoken words, but he couldn't stop the odd thought jumping in.

'That's good to know,' said Angie.

'Of course. I can set up some one-to-ones for you with Rebecca. She's our Clinical Psychologist.'

'Oh. So, I wouldn't be talking to you?' thought Angie, a fraction of second before saying, 'That would be great, thanks.'

'You can talk to me about it, Angie, but I'm not a specialist. I'd need to refer you to Rebecca. That would be the correct procedure. *What are you doing, you idiot?'*

'Sure,' said Angie, hesitantly, a little taken aback by the frustration in Sag's inner voice. 'I understand… It's just that you've been looking after Lilly for so long, Sag. I know you… and you know us better than anyone else here. I've never met Rebecca. I'm sure she's good at what she does but she doesn't know me. She doesn't know what I've been through. You do.'

The fight inside him: "Professional Sag" versus "Personal Sag" had now reached a brutal round. They were really slugging it out, trading blows like completely spent boxers. Both exhausted. Both floundering. And it was by the sheer will to win that "Personal Sag" finally got "Professional Sag" up against the ropes.

'The thing is, Angie...' thought Sag, with his head lowered, terrified to look her in the eye, the tiger scratching at the door of his guard hut. *'Now I know you like I do... I think you're the strongest, most wonderful human being I've ever known.'*

'Do you?' thought Angie.

'Yes, I do,' Sag took the deepest breath of his life. *'Why do you think I've been here for so long? Why do you think I've turned down other places I could have gone?'*

'I didn't know you had. Why have you stayed?'

'Because if I'd left, I wouldn't be able to take care of Lilly anymore and... well... I wouldn't see you again.'

Angie straightened up. And involuntarily sat back in her chair, putting an extra half a yard of distance between them.

But Sag wasn't finished. It was all flowing over the edge of the falls.

'Angie... it's only when I'm with you... that I don't feel alone. You're the only person I've ever met who's ever taken that feeling away.'

And then there was silence.

Neither of them spoke.

And neither of them was capable of a coherent thought.

'Jesus, Sag. I had no idea,' said Angie, finally. Then, encouraging him to lift his head, 'Sag.'

Sag looked up, hanging on the next word like a white-knuckled free climber on sheer rock, grasping the narrowest of ledges.

'I think you're a wonderful person. Really. Wonderful. But I think I need to get back to Lilly.'

And with that, Sag lost his fingertip grip on the cliff face and started to fall. He felt Angie brush past his hair on the way out of the bleak, beige consulting room.

Sag stayed, rubbing the raised, angry scar on the back of his right thigh.

NINE

Fury

A day after The Event.
Somewhere in Essex.

Eddie Cox's relationship with cocaine was probably the longest, most stable one he'd ever had. For as long as he could remember, he'd lived in a pressure cooker. Eddie was a thinker. And, while that had its advantages, taking him to where he was with relatively little attention from the law, it also came with a tendency to overthink. And that usually didn't end well, either for him or, more often, for someone else.

It was this level of introspection and worry that had kept his business successfully out of the helicopter spotlight, but it was also the reason why Eddie became obsessed with whatever drug he'd chosen at the time.

He'd ended up going nowhere with puff. What started out as weekend mischief and fits of giggles that went on for hours… turned into skinning up for breakfast, slacking off work, not washing very often and instant paranoia as soon as he took his first toke.

Ecstasy went a similar way. To begin with, it was all euphoria and release and brotherhood and feeling like he was part of something… but it had turned into trying to hold it down, popping sixteen in one night and the inevitable anxiety and depression that came with completely fucking up your serotonin levels.

And again… he wasn't getting much work done.

Then cocaine came along. And Eddie had found his drug. It meant he could target with laser-guided precision. And shut down the part of his brain that tipped healthy thinking over the edge. And, while it was never far from his mind, he was able to keep his fixation with the powder at bay for long enough to put in a decent week's work and figure out a longer-term path for himself and his organisation.

Yep, cocaine was his wonder drug.

Even with its downsides.

It had messed up his heart, for a start. There was a fine line between doing enough to get high and doing too much, too quickly and having his heart feel like it was going to jump out of his chest. Towards the end of a session, needing more and more each time to stay up there, chopping out a line that would wreck a bull, sucking it up a nostril then, as it trickled down the back of his throat and got to work, realising that shit, he'd really pushed his body over its limits this time.

Just like the last time.

Having to stand up and move, thumping his chest, telling it not to conk out on him, trying to use up the energy coursing through every muscle and sending his ticker into overdrive.

After years of doing that to himself week in, week out, it wasn't any surprise that it would catch up with him eventually. The price he paid were two heart operations to fix a madly irregular heartbeat. Once that had been sorted, while he was still sore and annoyed with himself, he'd managed to shelve the habit. But, well… it was his business, wasn't it? He had access to the uncut stuff. And it was free. On tap.

So, as soon as each op became a distant memory and he caught the powdery petrol smell in the air, his craving for a sharpener got the better of him. The mantra of "don't get high on your own supply" hadn't worked for Tony Montana. Why would it work for Eddie?

Then there were the days after the weekend before.

Being able to go at six-hundred miles an hour for two, sometimes three days straight was all fine and dandy while you were on it. But fucking hell, you didn't half drop when you had to stop. After some terrible decisions taken the day after, Eddie had at least been disciplined enough to force himself to have that day off.

Nothing got decided on a come-down day.

Today was a come-down day. Having spent the entire night wired to fuck, racking up line after line, each one longer and fatter than the one before. Downing a bottle and a half of brandy with lager chasers, simmering over the film playing in his head of Julie... HIS Julie letting another man shove his veined, hairy cock up her holiest of holies. The simmering had turned to lid-blowing steam when Jamie had come through with the fucker's address.

Repeatedly picking up his phone and scowling at the text sitting in his messages like an evil laugh at his expense, as the unwelcome dawn chorus of birdsong heralded first light… this morning, today, the start of his worst come-down day ever… his conclusion was simply that he had to make an exception to his rule.

In a state of rawness, feeling like his skin had been stripped, he'd retrieved a selection of weapons from the arsenal stashed around the house at the back of cupboards and drawers. So that now, amongst the residue on the glass table in front of him, was a forward-venting blank semi-automatic pistol that had been converted to fire live 9mm rounds, an antique five-shot revolver, a sawn-off… and his pride and joy: an Uzi - an open-bolt, blowback-operated submachine gun.

With a final look at Julie's picture on the mantlepiece, taken in the Seychelles a lifetime ago, and with his hair as wild as his mood, Eddie loaded the guns he felt the job deserved and headed out the door to his car.

Cocaine had also been a theme in Rick and Sarah's conversation in the cab, after the text had come in from Georgie. Rick blaming it again for his latest indiscretion, while to Sarah, his insidious habit was just another reason for him to fuck off out of her life.

Of course, Rick couldn't have prevented his mind from turning to his affair with Julie. It had been an unstoppable train of thought thundering along the track, from Georgie's warning about Eddie to an explanation of who Eddie was and who his wife was to Rick.

The reveal could never have happened at a good time, but having it rear its head at a moment when Sarah had just started to forgive him for the first affair (again), meant it really was the last nail in the cheap plywood casket of their marriage. The fact that it had come at that precise moment when she was allowing herself to feel a degree of empathy, made the humiliation cut a thousand times deeper.

She wasn't going to have it.

Not anymore.

The fucking cunt needed to go, kids or no kids.

They'd arrived home in what would normally have been fuming silence, but instead, Sarah's thoughts about all the misery she wished on him for the rest of his life and Rick's pathetic apologies and anger at getting caught again, joined together in an unholy union.

They'd put the kids to bed. And Rick had tried to start yet another night of reasoning and excuses. But this time, rather than entertaining any of it, Sarah had simply cried herself to sleep.

Rick woke to find Sarah crouching over him, all vicious and twisted. In the filtered tendrils of the morning light reaching through the blinds, her face and body appeared so contorted that, in Rick's half-conscious state, she looked demonic… possessed.

The fear made him parp under the duvet.

'Morning darling,' thought Sarah, wanting to disorientate her husband as much as possible knowing that thought, rather than speech, would have more of an impact. *'Did you sleep well?'*

'What the fuck? I can hear what she's thinking.'

Rick had woken with that temporary amnesia you get when something life-changing has happened, you've had a rough night and a very disturbing sleep.

'Oh yeah,' he thought, the double whammy of the thinking-out-loud thing and his marriage ending,

hitting him like two sledgehammers in the stomach, one after the other. 'What are you doing?'

'I've packed your clothes,' said Sarah, getting up to show Rick three bulging black bin liners by the window.

'Sarah let's just stop for a second. Let me wake up properly and we can talk about it.'

'There's nothing to talk about, Rick. You need to go.'

'Go where? I've got nowhere to go.'

'That's not my problem,' said Sarah. 'Take your shit and get the fuck out.'

'Sarah. Look. Just-'

'Just what, Rick? WHAT?' Sarah recomposed herself and forced the pitch and volume of her voice down to DEFCON 3. She wasn't going to get into an argument about it. There'd be no more chances. No wheedling his way out of this one. This time, she was keeping the high ground. 'What else is there to say? What can you possibly say that I haven't heard before?'

Rick was stumped, well out of his crease.

Eddie followed his sat nav to a quiet cul-de-sac in Blackmore. With its chippy, a ruby, a Chinese takeaway and three original Tudor pubs around a small village green, only a statue of St. George standing victoriously over a slayed dragon, slapped in the centre of the lawn, would have made it more English. Blackmore was a place that the word quaint had been invented for.

Through this enchanting English fairy tale, Eddie slowed to cruising and turned into the street he wanted, looking for the first number visible on the houses. That was even. He needed an odd number, so he switched his attention to the other side. Twenty-one... twenty-three... twenty-five.

This was it.

He turned the car at the end of the road and parked up opposite a modest semi, giving himself a clear line of sight to the front door.

He read Jamie's message again. It was still boring through him like acid as he checked the number in the little blue bubble: 25.

Eddie looked for signs of life, *'It's still early. Curtains are still closed. All good, if I can get it done quick enough.'*

Trouble was, that his usual antenna for a wrong move and a bad decision had stopped working in the small hours of the night before. The rage and the charly had fused that out to the point where now it didn't matter that he was in his own car, with his own plates, in a road where the slightest drama would cause blinds to twitch and heads to pop up.

He heaped some powder onto the back of his left hand, leant over, arched his back, closed one nostril with his right forefinger and hoovered it all up with two efficient sniffs.

Sarah opened the window and picked up the nearest bin liner, 'You can either take them down yourself or pick 'em up from outside. I don't give a shit.'

'Don't. Please. Sarah, just calm down and let's talk about it,' pleaded Rick, half in, half out of bed.

Sarah pushed the stuffed bin liner out the window.

'Sarah, for fuck's sake…'

She picked up the second and squeezed it through the window frame. Then the third, which was so big it got stuck on the handle.

In that state of anger that's infectiously funny to anyone watching who isn't involved, she wrestled with it so hard, the thin black plastic split, sending her off balance to the floor and a selection of Rick's socks and pants raining down onto the driveway below.

Rick was now out of bed and torn between putting on a pair of jeans and helping his wife up. After a split-second decision, he bent down, offering Sarah a supportive hand, only to have it smacked away with cat-speed reflexes.

Sarah leaped to her feet, surprising herself with the efficiency of her movements and a bizarre, tired thought flashed across her brain, a leftover from the flight home, *'I'm a fucking MINJAAAA.'*

'What?' thought Rick.

'Get. The. Fuck. Out,' said Sarah in a ferocious whisper, stepping to within an inch of Rick's nose.

Rick was a deer in the headlights. Frozen to the spot.

Until Sarah flanked him and started pushing his back towards the door. She got him to the top of the stairs, where he turned in protest, only to be pushed so hard he tumbled down the first few steps.

Instinctively, he twisted his body to try to regain some balance but each time he managed to get his feet in the right position, Sarah shoved him again.

He ended up on his arse at the foot of the stairs with the front door repeatedly bashing against his hip, as Sarah tried to open it and finish what she'd started.

The only threadbare, frayed plan Eddie had formulated was to simply walk up to the front door, ring the bell and wait for the bloke who lived there to answer it. If anyone else answered, he'd just ask for him by name.

What he hadn't predicted was to hear shouting and thumping coming from inside the house he was watching. He certainly didn't expect the first-floor window to open and to see three bin liners come flying out, one of them shredded and spilling its contents, what seemed to be a man's underwear drawer, all over the front garden.

What Eddie saw next was a figure being ejected backwards out of the front door. It was a bloke in a T-shirt and pants. Bed hair and barefoot. He came out so fast, his legs couldn't work quick enough to stop him toppling over the backs of his heels and onto his arse.

It was now or never.

Eddie picked up the Uzi from the passenger seat and, with the palm of his right hand, checked the magazine was in properly. Then he popped the driver's door open and got out.

The ground underneath him felt like it was moving.

Eddie realised that it had been a while since he'd been on his feet and he could suddenly feel the effects of the extraordinary amount of booze in his blood, only made manageable by the quantity of coke he'd snorted. It took a moment for him to steady himself enough to put one foot in front of the other.

And then the familiar red mist descended and Eddie powered up into looney-tunes mode. He strode across the street, raising the gun with his left hand and slotting it into his right. His finger now trembling on the trigger.

'RICKY?' Eddie bellowed as he walked.

Rick was just getting to his feet when he heard his name being shouted.

'What's this now, a fucking angry neighbour?' Rick thought out loud, as he turned towards the source of the interruption. *'The nosy cunt can just fuck off back inside and leave me alone.'*

Now Eddie had his attention, he just needed one final confirmation that he'd got the right man.

'Are you Ricky?' said Eddie from the middle of the road, close enough now not to have to shout.

'Yeah, I'm Ricky. Who the fuck are you?'

Rick's anger at his own situation overpowered any logical thought process about who this might be, as he peered through the sleep in the corners of his eyes, trying to focus on the man that was marching in his direction.

But then it occurred to him that it was the version of his name he'd only ever used when he was playing away from home.

And then it all clicked into place in a fraction of a second.

This wasn't a neighbour.

This was Eddie.

Fuck.

Before Rick even saw the gun in Eddie's hand, he turned back to Sarah, who was now distracted by their two boys, yawning and stretching as they padded down the stairs towards her. She was trying, and failing, to reassure them that everything was fine and they should go back to bed.

Gabby and Cal had been woken by the first round of raised voices. Sadly, it was a sound they were used to. And they'd followed the shouting to the foot of the stairs to find their dad lying in the driveway and their mum trying to keep him there.

Cal was now wailing behind Sarah. Gabby was trying to peek around his mum to see what kind of expression was on his dad's face, hoping he'd be laughing, that this was just some weird joke they were playing on each other.

Outside, Eddie raised the weapon and squeezed the trigger. Nothing happened. Rick's head, spinning on his neck between his escape route and Eddie, now saw what Eddie had in his hands.

'Sarah, let me back in, please,' said Rick with a primal level of panic he'd never felt before.

'Fuck off, Rick,' said Sarah, who couldn't see beyond him.

Rick launched himself at the front door, just as Sarah slammed it. He just managed to wedge a bare foot inside the frame, crushing his toes and bouncing the door back in Sarah's direction, catching her on the forehead. Both of them yelped from opposite sides but Sarah, even more incensed by the pain and the fact that her kids were now having to witness the whole sorry episode, found superwoman strength to barge the door back Rick's way.

On the pavement, Eddie was fiddling with the Uzi. He remembered that he'd never actually fired it before. In a country where the only people who had guns were armed response units and drug dealers, where do you practice shooting a submachine gun?

At first, he couldn't work out why it hadn't fired. His hand had been on the grip safety. So, it could only be… the selector lever. That was it. He flipped it from the S position and raised the barrel, but the tension in his hands squeezed the trigger while the gun was still on the way up, before he managed to aim it properly.

A spatter of rounds bounced up from the tarmac and peppered the front of Rick and Sarah's house. As the bullets hit the ground, they spun, turning each projectile into tiny, white-hot circular saws, scything through anything they came into contact with.

Rick's thigh was the first bit of flesh to take one. Entering the back of his leg, slicing through his muscle and sinew before shattering his femur and exiting through his knee cap. Others went through the front door, splintering the glass and the wood, grazing Sarah's hip and ricocheting around the hallway.

And then the world went quiet.

From where Eddie stood, he could see thick blood pouring from the gaping wounds on Rick's leg. Rick's eyes were swollen in shock; his mouth open with the incomprehensibility of what had just happened. Eddie could see a woman inside with a small child standing behind her and another tiny body lying crumpled at the foot of the stairs. There was a spray of blood, and other stuff that he couldn't make out, up the wall.

And then the red mist lifted.

Eddie sprinted back to his car, knowing heads were appearing in windows with their curtains now fully open.

Sarah didn't notice the blood seeping through her ripped dressing gown or the shards of glass embedded in her cheek. She was trying to fathom what the red, grey and white substances were that were now decorating the walls of her hallway.

She looked down to see Gabby lying unnaturally across the bottom step. Half his jaw was gone. One of his eyes had burst. And the other stared back at her, cloudy and lifeless.

TEN

Yearning

A day after The Event.
Somewhere in Cambridgeshire.

Angie and Lilly's drive home from the hospital had been dominated by daughter relentlessly grilling mother on precisely what had been said during her alone time with Sag.

Angie had been honest. She'd always been honest with Lilly, even when bad news had been followed by worse news. She figured it was the least she owed her kid and Angie's unbridled transparency and respect for Lilly's intelligence had blossomed a delicate bud into an open, colourful, self-assured young lady.

Lilly had wanted the ins and outs, in every last detail. And when she got it, she asked for it again, until Angie had repeated almost every sentence of the exchange at least twice.

Angie could feel Lilly's scrutiny having an interesting effect. Her initial reaction to Sag's emotional confession had been to bristle and detach. Bristle and detach - parry and move – it was a reflex she'd now committed to muscle memory whenever she encountered something in her life that broke her concentration on Lilly's.

But now, Angie felt herself softening as she replayed Sag's words over and over again, all the way home. And, being encouraged to do so by the person that mattered most, meant that Angie could bring her feelings to the surface for a much-needed breath.

'He is pretty cute, isn't he?' Angie had said to the windscreen.

'Cute? He's gorgeous, mum. That chiselled jaw. The kindness in his eyes. And... his-'

'His skin?'

'His skin!'

They said/thought the same two words in unison and their tiny corner of the universe, their little bubble inside Angie's car, filled with laughter.

While Lilly kept everything in her mind, thriving on the oxygen she could keep in her lungs for a fraction of a heartbeat longer, Angie found the conversation easier when she spoke out loud.

'You don't mind if I talk, do you?' said Angie.

'Of course not. Whatever's easier for you,' thought Lilly.

'Good. We can practice more when we get home. How long do you think it'll last?'

'I don't know, mum. I hope it's forever. I love it.'

Angie darted her eyes from the road to Lilly's face. And smiled at what she saw there, 'You really do, don't you?'

At home, they'd both then followed their usual routine when something profound had happened: sharing mum's big bed and giggling like schoolgirls until they fell asleep.

The following morning, Lilly found her mum in the kitchen putting the last of the breakfast things onto the table.

Angie looked up, all bright and shining in front of the dark clouds outside and the rain racing down the window behind her.

'Here she is. How are you feeling? It was a bit of a rough night, wasn't it?'

Lilly had been struggling to clear the mucus build up in her lungs. Sometimes it was so thick, it felt like glue. The crackle in her breathing and the lack of oxygen reaching her blood had woken them both at least half a dozen times. And, as usual, Angie was downplaying the inconvenience and exhaustion it had caused.

'Yeah. Sorry mum,' Lilly thought as she crossed the room.

'Shht. I've told you a thousand times… no apologies. It's not your fault. Now… how hungry are you? I'm making your favourite: toasted bagel with streaky bacon - American-style, avocado and srirrrrrachaaaa,' said Angie, chuckling with herself. 'I've been saying that word like that for so long, I can't say it any other way now.'

Lilly took her seat at the table.

'Is it a poppy seed bagel?'

'Ch-yeah, of course,' said Angie, breaking up the crispy bacon with her fingers and adding it with a flourish as the finishing touch. 'This thinking out loud thing is still working, then, isn't it?'

'Why, did you think it had stopped?' thought Lilly.

Angie brought their plates and put them down.

'Well, I wasn't sure. I got the bagels from the Jewish bakers up the road.'

'You've been out?'

'Yeah. It's late, baby. I just got back before the rain started. *God, it's tipping down now, that was lucky.* You've had a nice long lie in. And that's good, you needed it. But there are a lot of confused faces out there this morning.

'I tried ordering by thinking it, but the lady behind the counter looked at me like I'd just spat at her. It was only when I said it out loud that she got what I asked for. I couldn't work out if she'd heard my thought or not. Do you think it's only happening to some of us?'

'It's all over social, mum. Maybe there are some people that it doesn't work on, but from what I can see, it's happening everywhere.'

Lilly showed Angie her phone screen and scrolled quickly through post after post.

'I see what you mean. Let's see if there's any news about it.'

Angie hadn't quite been able to give herself up to relying solely on social networks for a competent appraisal of world affairs. So, she picked up the remote from the corner of the table and flicked on the TV.

Just as she found BBC News, the doorbell rang.

Angie looked at Lilly.

'You expecting anyone?'

'Nope,' thought Lilly, shaking her head.

As Angie got up to answer it, Lilly crossed everything she could, from her fingers to her feet.

Sag had had a rough night too. Returning to the claustrophobic flat he shared with two other nurses. "A compact little gem" was how the agent had sold it to them.

Dickhead.

Sag took a lot of pride from being in a profession that was always at the top of everyone's trusted list. And estate agents were firmly stuck at the bottom, weren't they? So, Mr. Slippery… take your "compact gem" and shove it up your sigmoid colon.

It had been all they could afford. And, as much as Sag would have given for a place of his own, he felt lucky to have found two people willing to share the cost. It was a necessary evil.

His flatmates were on shift, one of them on a double, so he had the place to himself.

Thank god.

He hadn't felt like contributing to the inevitable in-depth analysis of what was happening. He just wanted to be on his own, to process his epic fuck-up.

As lonely as he was, whenever he allowed himself to think about it, Sag had always been confused by how anxious he felt in other people's company. In those situations, all he wanted was to be on his own.

His longing for solitude never ceased to baffle him. It seemed so counterintuitive.

The little bit of therapy he'd tried, the only sessions he could afford, had pinpointed the cause of this seemingly masochistic tendency, to his childhood. Being the only offspring of two emotionally stunted, avoidant parents had fostered a number of self-defence mechanisms. Taking himself off, where no one could see him cry inside, being one of them.

Sag was grateful there was no one around to hear how he felt about himself. He replayed every second of his exchange with Angie, physically recoiling each time he remembered what he'd thought out loud.

'If this thing does last,' he thought, *'then I'm properly fucked. No more covering up my eternal embarrassment at my own behaviour. Nope. That's going to be well and truly out in the open. Everyone's going to know what a joke you are, Sag. What are you going to do now?'*

Sag's inner voice often switched to the third person at the tail end of an internal monologue, whenever he was telling himself off.

It turned abusive and frightening.

It was so aggressive that sometimes it even spilled out into speech. Too late to catch them, he'd realise that he'd involuntarily said the last few words of his thought process out loud, as if "Self-loathing Sag" had to break out of his mind and into the real world, to ram home the point.

It was still his voice, but it was a very dark version of him. Almost a different person... but not quite. He'd learned that it was someone he had to turn the tables on, to put in its place before it got too powerful.

'Stop it,' thought Sag's conscious brain. *'Just stop it. Give yourself a break. You were honest with her, that's all. That can't be wrong.'*

'You're kidding yourself. It was ridiculous and you're going to get fired. It's a disciplinary waiting to happen.'

Sag shook his head, hoping it would act like a splash of cold water in the face. He needed to put the brakes on and try to think more clearly about what he'd done and how Angie would be feeling about it.

And nothing was going to get solved that night.

So, he'd tucked himself into bed, drew into a foetal position and, with the covers tight around his neck, closed his eyes into a fretful sleep.

In the morning, Sag woke like he hadn't slept. But he must have, because his dream spells of being shamefully exposed had been more vivid and potent than usual.

It only took half a minute for the sick, fluttering feeling in his stomach to come back and work its way around his body, so it felt like all his muscles were shaking, even though they weren't.

His memory was unchanged.

Bollocks.

Sag rubbed his face with both hands before concentrating his fingers on his forehead, hoping that somehow the movement might encourage his brain to work a little more efficiently and focus on what needed to be done.

Work first.

He called the CF unit to be told that he was most likely being redeployed and that he needed to keep his mobile on to find out where.

But then, what else was he going to think about but Angie?

He was always a little kinder to himself in the mornings, so he dared to play out the scenario of what would happen if he followed up on his actions from the day before.

Could he call her?

Could he go see her?

Could he bring himself to tell her the same things again?

Would she have changed her mind?

Would she be more open to it today?

Or would any contact, of any kind, make her mind up, if she hadn't already decided, to report him for unprofessional conduct.

Right now, he might just get away with it.

Lilly might have persuaded her not to put in a complaint. But if he made another move... well they'd come down on him like a ton of bricks, wouldn't they?

But then there was Lilly's argument that she made so... poignantly. Life was short, wasn't it? If he didn't do it, he'd likely spend the rest of his life wondering what would have happened if he did.

So, IF he did... there's the question of how?

When you had something as heartfelt as this to say, it's almost impossible to put into a message.

Not being able to see her face and judge the nuances of her reactions on the phone wouldn't be good either. A phone call's too detached. It might come across as creepy.

No. If he was going to do it, he'd have to do it face to face.

Turning up at her home.

With everything that implied.

It was the only way... IF he decided to do something.

So, he played that out.

What would be the worst-case scenario?

She'd feel spooked, at best, that he'd looked up where she lived… and threatened, at worst, by him stepping way over the line into her personal space. She'd complain to the hospital. He'd be up on a disciplinary, with no leg to stand on and he'd probably never work in medicine again. The only pro being that he would have scratched the itch and he'd know once and for all that Angie would never be his future.

Fucking hell.

The worst-case scenario sounded horrendous.

And the tiger was back. Prowling around outside his hut. Enticing him to make a move by mimicking a harmless animal.

By the time Angie had got to the front door, it was raining so hard it was making a racket, bouncing high off the skylight above the hallway. Angie opened the door to see Sag disappearing into the deluge.

'Sag?' she called.

No response.

She tried again, lifting her volume over the drumming of the water, 'SAG!'

Sag forced his feet to stop moving.

He lifted his head over his shoulder, so Angie was just at the edge of his vision.

There were claws.

Big, sharp ones.

Now forcing their way through a crack in the door.

'I shouldn't be here,' said Sag.

'WHAT? I CAN'T HEAR YOU,' shouted Angie, stepping across the threshold, taking a few spears of sharp, heavy rain before moving back into the dry.

Sag raised his head a little more and rotated his body towards the house.

He was kicking out.

'I SHOULDN'T BE HERE,' Sag repeated with as much volume as he dared, trying not to sound too frustrated, petrified that the person who held his soul in their hands might read it as anger.

Angie took a long look at the drowning man at the end of her path.

'Sag, why don't you come in?' she said. 'You're soaked to the bone.'

Sag stood statue still in Angie's hallway, dripping awkwardly onto her rug. He could smell something delicious. What was it? Bacon. And toast. And an unfamiliar house smell. Freshly dried laundry and Angie's perfume. All of it combined to warm him instantly.

This was a real home.

It was the first time in his whole life that he'd ever known what one felt like.

The sound of the front door closing snapped a thought into his head, *'Well that's it. You've done it now. It's all or nothing from here, Sagaren.'*

Angie slid past him, avoiding the sopping wet material stuck to Sag's shoulders. He wasn't sure if she'd heard his thought or not. She hadn't responded to it. Maybe the sound of the rain on the skylight had saved him.

Angie had heard it.

She just didn't want to make him feel any more uncomfortable by acknowledging it.

'Jesus Sag. Didn't you bring a brolly? You're not even wearing a coat.'

Sag wanted to answer but nothing came out.

'Stay there. Don't get anything else wet,' Angie said, as she ran up the stairs.

Sag caught his reflection in the hallway mirror.

Fuck.

He looked like he'd been swimming with his clothes on.

Angie reappeared with a huge towel and a T-shirt.

'Here. It's the only thing I think I've got that'll fit you. Give me that and I'll dry it for you.'

And so it was that Sagaren Masih found himself undressing in the home of the woman he'd been infatuated with since he first laid eyes on her five years ago.

'When I woke up this morning, the last thing I expected to be doing today was this,' Sag thought as he peeled off his top.

'It's a bit of a surprise for me too, Sag,' said Angie, before a thought that she just couldn't help, popped in there. *'Your skin is beautiful.'*

It triggered a wave of desire in Sag like a tsunami rearing up as it reached the shallows.

'Fucking hell. I want to kiss this woman so badly. But I've got to slow down. No, not slow down, I've got to stop. Just put the T-shirt on.'

Sag had to wrestle the material down over his torso. It kept getting rolled up and stuck as the cotton met his damp body.

'Get. The. Fucking. T. Shirt. On.'

Angie watched Sag twist and turn and reach and repeatedly fail to grasp the bit of the shirt that was caught up the middle of his back. She let herself enjoy the moment until she couldn't let him wriggle anymore. She leant forward and reached behind him to calmly unfurl the material stuck between his shoulder blades.

Then looked Sag straight in the eyes.

Before tilting her head towards the heart of the house.

'Come on,' she said. 'Lilly will be pleased to see you.'

'Hi Sag,' said Lilly, like it was the most natural thing in the world to see him sit down at the family table while she was eating breakfast.

'Hello you,' said Sag. *'Why am I not surprised… that you're not surprised… that I'm here?'*

Lilly shrugged playfully. And only then did she look up to smile at the one person, apart from her mum, that she'd probably spent most of her time with since she could remember.

'Oh my god, Sag. You're drenched. Look at your hair! It's plastered to your face. It makes your head

look tiny. And what are you wearing? Mum, is that your night shirt?'

'It's all I've got, Lilly. Sag came out without a coat.'

'Or a brolly,' added Sag in Lilly's direction, watching her shake her head, enjoying translating her action into a single word: *'Twat.'*

Angie loved to watch the two of them together. She couldn't have asked for more in a relationship between her daughter and her first point of contact at the hospital. They spent so much time there, she felt unbelievably lucky to have had Sag assigned to Lilly.

She allowed herself a little sigh of contentment.

'Sag, can I get you anything? Are you hungry?'

'God no,' Sag laughed inside at the idea of food in the middle of all his turmoil. 'No, thank you, Angie. I'm good. I'm not hungry. Just… maybe some water?'

'Sure,' Angie said, pulling a glass out of the cupboard.

'What's happening at the hospital, Sag? Have you got the day off?' thought Lilly.

'Well, not really,' said Sag. 'I'm waiting for a call. They're redeploying me because of all the emergencies that are coming in. So, I might have to go soon. We'll see.'

'Well, you can't go to work looking like that, can you? Let me dry your hair.'

Lilly took a last bite of bagel and picked the towel out of Sag's hands. She draped it over him like a kid playing ghost with a sheet. And then looked up at her mum as Angie brought a glass of water to the table.

'He's here!' Lilly mouthed, wide-eyed and excited, forgetting the thought was out loud.

Angie mouthed back.

'I know!'

'I heard that,' said a muffled voice under all the fluff.

And with that, Lilly started rubbing with all her strength, sending Sag's head right and left, the towel sliding off his face for just long enough for Angie to see a relaxed, beaming smile on Sag's face.

Lilly started coughing. She was just coming out of yet another flare up of Bronchiectasis and hadn't done her daily mucus clearing yet. All the effort with the towel had made her breathless. The phlegm felt extra sticky in her lungs and no matter how much she coughed, she couldn't get it out.

Angie was calm enough. Even though she hated it, she'd dealt with this before. She immediately went to the medical cabinet in the kitchen.

Sag was even quicker on the draw. He pulled the towel off his head and threw it onto the next chair.

'Could you bring Lilly's nebuliser please Angie? Some alcohol gel, you should have some salbutamol there too and four millilitres of hypertonic sodium chloride.'

'Err… hypertonic…' said Angie as she quickly surveyed the contents of the cupboard.

'Sorry… saline.'

'Ah, yes. Saline. Got it.'

Angie dropped it all onto the table.

Sag took the gel and rubbed his hands with it.

He opened a vial of salbutamol and squeezed the liquid into the nebuliser chamber.

'It's OK, Lilly. I've got your nebuliser. We're going to use the salbutamol first. You know what that is. It'll take away any nasty effects of the saline. Just take the mouthpiece and breathe in the mist. That's it, good girl, just like you're used to. Well done. Now for the saline.'

Sag checked the expiry date of the salt solution and saw that it was fine. He reloaded the nebuliser and repeated the breathing process with Lilly until she gave him the nod that it was working, that the phlegm was starting to change its consistency.

'Do you have a…' whispered Sag to Angie before realising she was already there, holding the tissue Lilly needed.

Ten minutes later and Lilly was finally able to bring up the glue in her lungs.

While the episode was familiar, the way it was handled was new to Angie. She'd seen how good Sag was with Lilly many times over at the hospital. But this was happening in her home, in Lilly's home. And that made a difference.

Sag had stayed close, calm, in control and there for her daughter, through the whole thing.

And he always would, wouldn't he?

So, it occurred to her: who else would give Lilly the care and commitment that this man was showing? That he'd shown for most of her child's life. And do it all out of love. For Lilly. And for her.

And the perfect chocolate mirror-glazed skin?

Well, that would just be the cherry on the icing on the cake, wouldn't it?

ELEVEN

Hope

A month after The Event.
Unknown location.

If the world wasn't divided enough already, it was forced apart like opposite poles on a magnet after The Event.

That's what everyone called it.

It wasn't like a pandemic. It wasn't a virus you could see under a microscope. It wasn't a thing you could point to in the body and give it a name. Not to begin with, anyway.

So, after a few weeks of sharing and blogging and vlogging and influencing… everyone seemed to collectively agree, over the ones and zeros of the planet's digital network, that "The Event" was broad enough to cover it, whether your religion was magic or science, but specific enough for everyone to know exactly what you meant when you said it.

Even after its redundancy, speech was too much of a habit to drop straight away. Instead, a hybrid emerged, with people using their thoughts to punctuate a conversation or emphasise a point.

The deep, the dark and the brutally honest in our minds became open season for anyone close enough to hear and judge us by.

An organisation sprung up that actually called themselves the Thought Police. And boy, did they have a field day: able to wallow permanently in the bubbling hot mud of outrage; never off duty.

People took to wearing headphones. The closed cup ones seemed to work best, smothering thoughts in music so they were all but indecipherable as they spilled out into the 3.46 metre radius around each of us.

Seeing them on so many people's heads is what gave an audio engineer the idea of trying to adapt noise-cancelling technology to analyse the sound waves of thoughts and generate an opposite wave cancelling them out before they reached the outside world. Someone else was working on a device that could reflect the thought frequencies back into the brain. But so far at least, there hadn't been a breakthrough.

Headphones also blocked other people's thoughts from interrupting our own, but it made for a nightmarish soundtrack of conflicting beats, chords, melodies and voices every time we were forced together in closed spaces. Any journey on public transport was like being in an angry orchestra pit while they were tuning up and arguing with each other.

Then there were headphone-haters. Broadcasters, they called themselves. They were purists who stuck fast to the idea that everyone's thoughts SHOULD be heard. And if you were wearing headphones, well that just meant you had something evil to hide.

Headphoners avoided them like their souls depended on it, because the more militant Broadcasters were known to rip off headsets and force themselves on you by thinking loudly and proudly in your direction.

The speed at which these groups formed themselves was impressive. Maybe it wasn't surprising. With every global virus that had sent us into another meltdown, we'd had plenty of practice sorting ourselves into the far ends of the opinion spectrum. The world had turned black and white. And if you weren't in either camp, then you weren't really considered to be anywhere.

And so it was that half of us were desperate for a cure and took to marching in the streets, protesting that someone, somewhere needed to do something.

And the other half, who saw the new normal as a heroic transition, with everyone forced to advertise their true feelings as clearly as a flashing neon sign above their heads, celebrating the fact that you no longer had to take a calculated guess at who was good, bad or ugly.

Some clever sod from that side of the fence made a fortune setting up the world's first Think-Easy: a dive bar where "all thoughts were welcome". And a well-known Swedish movie director announced a new genre of filmmaking called "Ren" a partially scripted, partially improvised style where actors had to communicate with each other without opening their lips.

But, in the main, people slid into an ever more isolated state, as they distanced themselves from the crucifying judgement of others and the ones you thought you could trust became fewer and further between. All it took was a slip of the mind and even those with, what used to be considered genuine integrity, lost the high ground immediately.

With everyone's truth constantly exposed, only those with absolutely no agenda or purely benevolent intentions could form lasting relationships.

So, in short, some needed to hide.

Others rejoiced in having that option taken away.

Eddie Cox opened his eyes to a halo of bright light above his head. It took him a while before he understood where he was. The dank, gagging stench of "rotting vegetation and fox shit soup" brought it flooding back, that the circle of light was nothing angelic. It was the opening of the filthy, pissy culvert he'd spent the night in.

How he'd managed to evade the cops for twenty-eight days straight was a miracle.

They'd forensically cleared his house of evidence. Two guns had been dusted and bagged. Boxes of ammunition confiscated. The remnants of his coke binge photographed and samples taken.

And then, of course, there was the not insignificant problem of, if they knew, no one would be able to keep Eddie's whereabouts a secret.

Even the darkest, most deeply scarred villains, the ones who'd rather have their fingernails ripped out than shop one of their own, wouldn't be able to help themselves. If the knowledge was in there, it would come out, straight onto a PACE recorder in an interview room.

Armed with the new ability to tell instantly if someone was lying or withholding information, there weren't many organisations in the world that had leapt on the thinking-out-loud phenomenon with more enthusiasm and glee, than law enforcement.

It hadn't taken long for them to find the car, abandoned on a country lane about half a mile from the first safe house Jamie had organised, after Eddie had woken him with the update.

If Eddie had slept, even for just an hour, if his nostrils weren't still caked with coke… if he wasn't in a panic about ANPR cameras picking up his plate as soon as he got anywhere near civilisation… he might have taken Jamie's advice and left the car by a busy road the other side of Dartford, then doubled back... sending the old bill on a goose chase south.

But he wasn't thinking straight, was he?

Quite the opposite.

His mind was as snapped and limp as a broken cock.

The area surrounding Eddie's car was now royally fucked.

Coppers were going house to house.

And there was a helicopter in the sky.

Eddie had been forced to scarper from his first refuge, without giving Jamie enough time to sort another set of wheels.

So, legging it, it was. Literally.

From now on, he was on foot.

Georgie had been taken in for questioning twice, the police singling her out as the person most likely to crack after they'd hacked her phone and retrieved the deleted data, revealing the text she'd sent Rick. She was useless to them, though. She had no idea where Eddie was, Jamie had made sure of that.

Because now, not even Jamie could know what dark drainage hole Eddie had managed to crawl into.

He'd spent the first few days lining up more safe houses and dropping burner phones and packages off at all of them in case Eddie showed.

But they weren't safe for long, given the scrutiny Jamie was under. They didn't even have to tail him. All it took was another round of interviews at the cop shop. The more Jamie tried not to think about where they were, the quicker the addresses appeared in his head and then they were out… out loud. The locations were then listed and raided within hours.

Eddie had only just managed to avoid them at the last one by jumping out of a first-floor bedroom window, landing awkwardly on a kid's plastic Batmobile parked on the patio that had shot sideways with his foot still caught in it, twisting his ankle and making him fall hard on his hip. The only reason he'd escaped, sprinting on quickly swelling joints with cocaine killing the pain, was because the over excited cops hadn't waited for the dog unit to get there before battering the front door in.

Jamie hadn't been held for obvious reasons. Essex Police were hoping he'd eventually lead them to their prize. Both Jamie and Eddie knew it. So, they'd been forced to scrap the idea of contact of any kind. They couldn't run the same risk twice.

Eddie's clock was all over the news. If he tried to use a card, it would light up somewhere on their network. ATMs were out for the same reason. If he walked into a shop or turned up at a food bank, he'd run the gauntlet of being ID'd. If he pulled his gun out and held up a chippy, well that would be more than a breadcrumb, wouldn't it? And, he didn't have any cash left.

So, Eddie was back in the Stone Age. With no ability to hunt or gather for his supper. The mighty oak that was Eddie Cox had taken to hanging out in alleyways behind takeaways, digging through wheelie bins for scraps.

With the coke long gone, without pain relief or medical attention and the constant pressure to stay on the move, Eddie was in agony. The final blow to his body's ability to function as he needed it to, came when his heart decided that now would be the perfect time to flip back into atrial fibrillation.

Eddie hauled himself up into the only position he could find that his ankle and hip could tolerate, putting his weight on his good foot and pressing his back into the side of the concrete tube he was in.

He didn't have to look in a mirror to know that his skin, where it wasn't stained with dirt, was a lighter shade of grey. The rapid changes in his heartbeat made every cell of his body feel colourless and inert. Putting one foot in front of the other would have been difficult enough without his weight on one of them sending a lightning bolt up to his brain.

He lifted the hood of the manky sweatshirt he'd found on a deserted building site and stumbled his way out into the morning.

He needed transport.

He figured that getting out of the country was his only hope. Once he was across the water, disappearing into the continent wouldn't be easy but at least his face wouldn't be all over the media.

For that to happen, he needed a shed load of luck.

The first stroke of that had come when Jamie had used a burner phone to send a single text that he'd posted his passport to the Alamo… the last safe house on their list. And Eddie had collected it minutes before the door was bashed in.

It had been a few weeks, so the feds may well have put border control on alert. But using his passport once… if they'd been slack and hadn't coordinated their forces… if he didn't go the obvious route down to Dover… but went for Harwich instead… well, all things considered, given everything he was facing… it seemed like the least shit option of the few shitty options he had left.

It took Eddie the best part of the day to limp to the bus station at Chelmsford, where he discovered there were three different buses he needed to take to get to the port. Not the quickest route, but the least risky.

He tried begging for change to scrabble the fares together, but no one was having any of it. Aside from the state Eddie was in and the smell he was radiating, most people were wearing headphones, so his pleas for compassion went unheard or ignored. And anyway, we'd all stopped giving the homeless spare change since we'd stopped carrying spare change.

Not a penny.

In three hours.

And the more he put his face in someone else's, the more chance he had of being recognised.

There was only one thing left to do.

Fuck the bus.

And there was his second stroke of luck: the train station was less than a hundred yards away.

If he did what he was thinking of doing and he was quick enough… if he could make it onto the ferry to Holland before the flags went up... maybe it would be OK... maybe his luck would hold for one last stroke.

And so it was that Eddie tapped his card on the contactless point on the ticket machine and waited to board the next train to the coast.

The intricate aromas of a grand Punjab Thali-in-the-making wafted to Angie's nostrils. Sag was doing it again. For no other reason than it was a Wednesday. He was celebrating another day in the company of the two human beings he wanted to be around more than any other, by launching himself into the complex process of preparing no fewer than ten different dishes for lunch.

Sag had learned to cook by being starved of his mother's attention.

The leave that St. Peter's allowed the boarders was usually no longer than a week at a time... ten days at the most. With Sag's two-day journey and the severe repercussions of having the next leave cancelled or even expulsion from the school if he was late back, his father dismissed most of his holidays as not worth the effort of coming home.

Then there were the school limits on the amount of contact the pupils could have with their parents, claiming too much made them homesick. Even birthday visits from family were strictly forbidden.

It was all in the college rule book.

So, it was only the longer winter break through December and January that Sag got any real time with his mother.

She always seemed pleased enough to see him. Although he could never quite read her fully. He often wondered what was lying there underneath. When she smiled, he always thought he could see sadness behind it. The edges of her mouth never quite turned up the way he wanted them to.

Seeing as she was always in the kitchen, that's where Sag wanted to be, even if he had to regularly brush off her impatience when he insisted on helping and messed it up.

He'd usually be relegated to the chore tasks like washing the rice, peeling the potatoes, chopping the tomatoes. He didn't care. It made him feel useful to her. And he divided his concentration between the stuff he could do with his eyes closed and closely watching the way she spiced every dish and timed everything, so it all came together at once.

Sag's relationship with Angie, by any normal measure of together time, would have been sceptically defined as a whirlwind before The Event. But because every thought was out loud and the start point was always considerate, caring, respectful of the other person, they'd got extremely close, extremely quickly.

There was no tension, no worries about how the other person felt. Back stories, wounds from the past and any insecurities were communicated instantly and a reassuring, supportive, loving response came back just as rapidly.

Their "honesty knob" was stuck at eleven.

And that enforced level of candour, between anxious people who wanted to give each other exactly what they needed, meant that two fragile human beings, who'd each been dealt a bad hand, were finding out that, together, in the new normal… they were invincible.

There was also never any doubt about how much Sag cared about Lilly. Something that fed Angie's soul to see.

Lilly was just happy to see her mum happy, now able to share the strain that she brought to their micro-family. It eased her conscience and she could feel her life force being drip-fed by watching the two of them together.

There was the odd naughty thought one had about the other when the mood took them, that crept out within Lilly's earshot.

Cringe.

But that was something they'd all learn to live with. Lilly knew that her understanding made that easier for them. And it was no price to pay for her mum's contentment.

Angie had just finished the extra training all airlines were giving their pilots and crews and was due back in the air at the weekend. The aviation industry had quickly worked out how to navigate their way through it. They refused to be caught on the ground with their landing gear and their pants down again.

Complimentary and compulsory headphones and ear plugs were being issued on all commercial flights and stewards were being taught the new procedures, as well as how to deal with anyone who refused to wear either before take-off or, far more importantly, mid-air. There were to be no exceptions. And it would be enforced rigidly. No ear defenders, no fly. And the penalties were purposefully harsh.

The Cystic Fibrosis Unit had reopened after three weeks. Just enough time to implement new social distancing protocols. A four-metre rule had been worked out relatively quickly with so many medical brains on the problem. And this was the crucial factor in allowing Sag to continue as Lilly's principal carer.

To begin with, they couldn't quite work out how they'd manage to keep their new relationship a secret while Lilly was in the hospital for treatment. Sure, they could keep their minds focused on the medical side of things, but it would be hard to keep that up a hundred percent for any extended period of time.

They'd be having to act like Oscar-winners all day long and that would bring a whole heap of unwelcome stress. Some informality would spill out at some point. And if it was witnessed, especially by a bureaucrat, well then Sag would be up in front of the Trust having to explain himself.

But now, with the four-metre rule in place, Sag could be present while the specialists spoke to Lilly. And all he had to do was to keep his mind off the personal side of things when he interacted with the other staff on the team.

As the unit opened, Sag had rescheduled Lilly's annual review and they'd been able to get through it without any hiccups. Not from a thinking-out-loud perspective, anyway.

Distancing had been tested and optimised at breakneck speed in the NHS because of the complaints that had begun raining down on the regulatory boards about consultants and nurses being abrupt and insensitive towards their patients.

Every bleak and weary thought a doctor had about a patient's chances of their particular situation not ending well, were spilled out onto hospital beds up and down the country. The ability to deploy a tactful bedside manner had vanished overnight.

Mental health took a nosedive as psychologists inadvertently told the vulnerable in their care precisely what they were thinking: in some cases that there was little hope of them ever changing, that they'd seen it all before and were as tired of their job as an assembly line worker putting the same small part into a bigger part of a bigger machine all day every day for thirty years straight.

And the General Medical Council were having a nightmare dealing with the plethora of NHS staff under investigation for sexual misconduct, overstepping the line with patients, their carers or other members of staff.

At the top of the organisation, there was a genuine concern that they wouldn't be able to cope if the brain drain carried on, as more and more consultants' positions were under review for having thoughts that would never have come to the surface if it hadn't been for The Event.

The last straw came when one of the country's leading paediatricians had to be suspended, pending an investigation, for multiple complaints from concerned parents about him having loud fantasies about no fewer than eight children in his care.

There was no guidance in place for this. And what was happening in the health service was happening in every other workplace across the world too.

Politicians and lawyers had to debate the issue of whether an out-loud-thought was the same as the spoken word.

A pin-sharp example was if someone had a racist moment in their minds. Should it be dealt with in the same way as the hate-crime of actually saying it out loud?

It was a fascinating discussion.

From one side it proved a person was a racist and they should be dealt with accordingly but from the other perspective, it was argued, people have disturbing thoughts all the time but recognize them as disturbing and dismiss them accordingly.

From one point of view, if someone had a sexual thought about a child, they were clearly a paedophile, while the opposing view was that even if someone had those thoughts, maybe due to being abused themselves as children, but resisted the urge to act on them, shouldn't that be deemed personal progress, rather than punishable by prison and having their mugshot added to the Sex Offender's Database? Shouldn't they be applauded for dealing with their own trauma in a way that didn't continue the cycle and hurt anyone else?

The debate would rage on for months.

And social distancing was a lot quicker to implement than getting a law passed, so it was the first place the NHS went, to save the expertise they'd invested so much time and money in.

After all, people weren't going to stop getting sick and who else was going to do the job?

Of course, the new rule brought its own issues. Four metres was quite a distance. Beds on wards were stripped to a handful. Consultations had to take place in bigger rooms, usually in corridors or deserted waiting rooms. Patients had to be spared their doctor's sometimes savagely honest opinions and the medical professionals needed protection from having any inappropriate thoughts overheard.

Sag and Angie knew the rules could change at any moment. It had only been a month and the phenomenon wasn't understood at all. The more research that was done, the more we got to the root of where it was all coming from and how it affected the body, the more likely different guidelines would be put into place.

For now, Sag could still be in the room, far enough away so his thoughts were his own but close enough to hear the words of the doctor. And Angie could easily keep her focus on the topic of her daughter's health.

But they both suspected that Sag's time at Addenbrooke's as Lilly's CF Clinical Nurse Specialist couldn't last forever.

Unequally… more excruciatingly… given the devastating results of Lilly's latest review, neither of them knew how long she had left.

They were all too aware that the decision of whether Sag should find another post before their involvement leaked out, might not need to be taken at all.

As his train pulled into Harwich International, Eddie Cox scoured the station for signs of the wrong people.

He waited for the train to come to a stop before hauling himself out of his chair. There was no way he'd be able to stay on his feet if the carriage jerked too violently.

He tentatively pressed the open button, as if doing it gently would make the doors' hydraulics quieter. Steadying himself on the handrail, he leant forward and put half a head out.

It was late. And the platform was dead.

Wait.

Two blokes were getting off.

They looked Dutch. If you'd asked Eddie what Dutch looked like, he wouldn't have been able to tell you. Maybe it was blind optimism, but to him they just did.

He stepped out into the orange and lime of a world lit by sodium vapour and surrounded by industry.

The black, salty sea air smelt like the edge of freedom. As clichéd as it was, he could actually taste it.

Eddie hung back, waiting for the men to disappear before making slow, horribly uncomfortable progress to the end of the platform, stopping now and then to rest against the brickwork when his blood pressure bottomed out, his head started spinning and his legs threatened to give way from under him.

He followed the signs to the ferry terminal and descended into the exit. No inspector. No guard. No barriers. No need for a ticket. Eddie flinched like he'd just been stabbed, as he remembered the moment he'd touched his card on that machine.

'Don't torture yourself. You didn't want any grief. Fuck it, it's done now. Just get yourself on a boat.'

He had no idea when the ferries ran. He hadn't thought that bit through either. He'd just needed to put one foot in front of the other in the right direction.

So, as he got closer to the port, he heaved with relief to see a huge Stena Line logo parked behind the buildings. He scanned a timetable on the wall.

This one was leaving at 11 pm.

Fucking result.

'Just one last stroke of luck, please… with a tired, disinterested passport check…'

A light beamed into Eddie's eyes so powerfully it nearly knocked him off his feet.

Deep, violent screams from behind his back made him instinctively pull out his 9mm, the one gun he'd managed to keep hold of.

But then he knew what this was, didn't he?

Fuck, they'd been right on it.

It had only been a couple of hours since he'd used his card.

And they'd guessed right.

Cunts.

This was it.

So. Fucking. Close.

He kept the gun low as he turned to face yet more lights punching him in the head, taking big hits wherever he looked.

If he raised his gun now, they'd shoot first and he needed time to process what he wanted to do.

As he adjusted, he could just make out the business end of four, maybe five G36 assault rifles trained right between his eyes.

'ON YOUR FUCKING KNEES!' came bellowing out of the darkness behind the glare.

Eddie could barely stand anyway, so he obliged, not even flinching as his kneecaps impacted the tarmac.

'PUT THE GUN - ON THE FLOOR - SLOWLY.'

The copper's words were shouted at the pace he wanted Eddie to comply.

Now, this is where it got interesting for Eddie.

His gun was a quick way out, wasn't it? And he didn't want to give up that option right away.

'PUT THE FUCKING GUN ON THE FLOOR!'

This time, the pace of the order was delivered like a railgun on a fighter jet.

Eddie slowly moved his right hand, his finger creeping to the trigger, before he quickly brought the weapon up as far as his own neck and jammed it under his jaw.

The G36s twitched.

This would at least give him a few more moments to think.

'Eddie. Put the gun down. You don't have to do this. It doesn't have to end here,' said the same copper's voice at a more respectful volume.

The sudden tenderness of it made Eddie cry.

He felt his body and his mind melting as the last four weeks were suddenly released.

Unseen, on Eddie's diagonal, a uniform with a taser got within range.

Eddie forced his quivering bottom lip to be still.

'You're Eddie Cox. Stop fucking shaking.'

His grip on the gun tightened and he shoved it harder into his chin, as though that would make a difference if he decided to let the bullet go.

But this was enough for the taser to be deployed.

Two fishhook probes pinned themselves to Eddie's chest and stomach, sending fifty thousand volts through his system.

Eddie immediately lost his gun as his fingers stiffened and he dropped backwards onto his heels.

In the crackle of electricity coursing everywhere, his mind catapulted him back to throwing dirt on his wife's coffin, sleeping in a drain, begging for money, eating from a bin… and the sight of a little kid's brains up the wall of a family home.

In the last second before he lost consciousness, Eddie's final hope was that the taser would fry his failing heart there and then.

Lilly had grown a lot weaker over the last few weeks. Her review had shown that her decline in lung function had accelerated. And no one could tell them why. There were so many factors at play. Everyone's inflammatory profile was different. It could be genetic. Even though she had a big appetite, her body wasn't able to retain the nutrients a normal person would from eating. It could be because girls and women were prone to suffer more. All the pulmonary problems she'd had over the years. The recurrent bouts of pneumonia. And now her emphysema was in the most serious state of all:

Stage four.

As her alveoli broke down, her bronchial tubes had started to collapse, trapping air in her lungs and making her chest puff out. Breathing was now such a problem that she found it almost impossible to sleep.

The news that Lilly needed a new set of lungs had knocked Angie for six.

Sag had put her on the waiting list. Average time with the NHS was eighteen months. But he knew Lilly would be prioritised as a person with more life ahead of her than others.

And so it was.

They were playing the waiting game.

All Angie and Sag could do was their best to keep her cheerful.

'Grub's up,' called Sag, as he arranged the table with makki di rotis, palak paneer, sarson ka saag, lachha parathas and basmati rice, even fluffier than mother used to make.

Angie leapt from her laptop and gave Sag a squeeze before sitting down hangrily. Sag joined her, unusually pleased with his efforts, excited to provide them both with the food of his childhood. Again.

Lost in the purity of their moment, they almost forgot about Lilly. Almost. A split second into it and they both looked at each other and then towards the empty stairs.

Angie opened Lilly's bedroom door to find her perched on the edge of her bed wrestling with a long-sleeved top and sounding like she was hacking up one of her internal organs.

'Baby, let me help you,' said Angie, rushing in while calling downstairs. 'SAG, CAN YOU BRING THE NEBULISER?!'

Lilly's cough broke and she grabbed a bowl from the bedside table, dispensing a thick lump of mucus into it.

'It's OK, mum. I think that's got it.'

'Good,' thought Angie, stroking Lilly's hair. *'No rush, but if you're hungry, Sag's cooked us one of his specials.'*

'I heard. And yeah, I'm starving. I'm Hank Marvin.'

Angie laughed through moist eyes.

'Do you know who he was?'

'Nah, haven't got a clue. Wait, was he a singer or something?'

'Close. He was a guitar player. He was in a band called The Shadows. Where did you get that name from?'

'TikTok,' thought Lilly. *'The Shadows. They sound scary.'*

Angie shook her head with delight at Lilly's innocent assumption.

'I suppose they do. But they weren't. Not at all.'

Sag arrived at the bedroom door and was pleased to see that he wasn't needed anymore. He wasn't sure whether to go back down or wait. Angie and Lilly looked like they were having a moment and he didn't want to interrupt.

'Mum?'

'Yes, baby?'

'I'm so happy for you.'

'What do you mean? Why?'

'I'm happy that you're happy. You've got Sag now.'

Angie's eyes glittered while she scanned her child's face.

'We've got Sag now. We. Us. We've got Sag now, haven't we?'

'Yeah, we have,' thought Lilly, barely able to hide the aching pathos her comment was loaded with. She glanced up to see Sag peering around the doorframe.

She beckoned him in.

Sag got as far as the middle of the room before his tear ducts opened.

He thought about leaving. He didn't want Lilly to see him break. Or to know what he was thinking about her chances of getting what she needed before it was too late.

But Lilly made up his mind for him.

'Don't go, Sag. And don't worry. It'll be alright.'

Which set Angie off too.

So, Lilly held them both. A scrawny arm around each of their heads as they knelt next to her bed, sobbing.

She looked out the window to the sun.

She'd never seen it looking more yellow.

Sag and Angie felt her chest gently rise and fall as Lilly took the deepest breath she could.

ABOUT THE AUTHOR

S. A. Sarky divides their time between London, New York, Vienna and Andalusia.

Printed in Great Britain
by Amazon